Scruffy's Discovery

Gemma Murdoch-Smith

To my special friend June, a little bookworm

Chapter 1

For as long as I can remember we had lived in London. All my school friends were there, along with the house and bedroom I grew-up in. My room's decoration had changed over time, perfected by me, of course. Some of my favourite posters, now, though, were beginning to look a bit worn-out around the edges. The wall art poster of my favourite singer, standing with her blonde hair blowing as she held her guitar was also looking a bit old fashioned now.

Although I was reasonably happy at home, something had changed recently and felt different. My mum and dad seemed to be arguing more. The atmosphere in the house was not quite the same either. Last week I had walked into the sitting room and found my mum sitting on the sofa crying, with red and wet cheeks. She was pretending not to, but I could tell she had been. As I came into the room, she quickly wiped them on her sleeve, perhaps thinking I wouldn't notice. My dad sometimes called her 'worryguts', as she could often worry or cry about problems that he did not feel were problems, but she would never really discuss what the issues were with me.

My big brother also seemed to be staying out later with his friends and told me he didn't like being in the house as it was 'boring'. One of my friends said that was because Robbie was 'becoming a typical teenager,' but I felt there was something more to it than that. Anyway, why should 'becoming a teenager' cause him to think that?

I wasn't surprised, then, when one day on coming back from school, my mum said she needed to talk to us about 'something,' and sat my brother and myself down in the sitting room. I remember holding my breath so I could carefully listen to every word.

"Lizzy and Robert," she said. "We are going to move house very soon and things are going to be quite different at home." Well, that didn't seem so bad, did it? Lots of people move houses all the time. She then said "It's going to mean moving quite a long way away and changing schools." I was so worried about my mum as her voice was gradually cracking up. Her blue eyes were filling with tears she was trying to hold back, trying to prevent them from spilling out. I knew that each sentence spoken was becoming harder for her to say, so I smiled as hard as I could to show that we could deal with that. She then said, "and Daddy is not going to be with us quite as much as he usually is." As she made this statement, those tears came trickling down her cheeks again. She tried hard to quickly wipe them away. I wasn't sure what exactly that would mean, and what the reason was for this, but I just thought I'd keep quiet in case there was anything left to say.

"You still love Daddy, though, don't you?" I asked.

"Of course," my mum said, smiling a little. I quickly tried to think what the best thing to say back was. I looked at my brother, who just looked angry, and like he was going to shout something out.

"So," I quickly jumped in. "Would you like a cup of tea Mum?" At this, she laughed.

"No LIzzy, but I'll make one for us all if you'd like one." With that she went off to the kitchen. My brother looked at me as though I was stupid.

"Well that ruins everything," he said, "including all the plans I had with my friends for the summer holidays, I hate parents sometimes." With that, he stormed off and slammed his bedroom door.

When my mum came back with a cup of tea for us all, we sat and watched the news on TV. I didn't really know what to say, in case it made matters worse, so just kept quiet. Robert's teacup remained full, and I thought I 'd wash it up, so he wasn't disturbed with questions about why it hadn't been drunk. I didn't want to upset my mum further, so just let her talk, and she asked me what we would like for dinner. I told her anything would be ok, so we agreed on fishfingers and beans (I also thought that would keep my brother happy). After sitting through a quiet dinner with an angry faced brother, I went on to wash- up some cups, did some homework (which I couldn't concentrate on) and then went to bed.

That night was so hard to sleep. I had so many questions flying around in my head. Why were we moving soon? Why would dad not be around so much? What would it be like without my friends? What would the new place be like? Would I make new friends? I was so worried about my mum as she seemed so upset as well. I wondered whether I should tell my brother off for slamming his door, but eventually I didn't think it would be worth it, and hopefully the anger would be gone in the morning. I pictured his furious face, the hairstyle went well, with spikes of it sticking up using that shiny hair gel he likes so much. Then I thought maybe his anger was really a way of expressing his upset, so I should be a little more understanding with him too.

Chapter 2

The next morning, I went to school unsure of how I was feeling. Normally I loved Wednesdays as we had Geography teaching, and my favourite teacher was there. I looked forward to the games' lessons on that day too, although I never seemed to be in the team that won. On arriving at school, I looked out for my friend Isabelle. Her blonde hair normally stuck out from everyone else's heads. This was lucky as she also was quite short and could disappear into crowds. On arriving in the classroom, I saw her sitting in the middle row and immediately grabbed the desk next to hers.

"I'd bagged this place for you," she whispered. The morning lessons seemed to take ages to get through, and I couldn't wait for the breaktime bell to ring so I could talk to Isabelle and see what she thought about everything. As soon as the bell rang everyone got up and scraped their chairs on the floor with a loud screech. Max the bully banged his big body past me, deliberately. I shouted at him to be more careful. He gave me that 'don't mess with me' look. I looked back at him, giving as sweet a smile as I could.

"Please just remember you're a lot bigger than us." As I said that, some of the boys laughed, so that put him in his place, as he could be horrible.

"So?" Max said, and walked off, sticking his head up in the air. I hooked my arm into Isabelle's and quickly walked with her out of the classroom to get to the busy corridor and then into the playground. We made our way towards our favourite area to sit on 'our wall,' and sat down arm in arm.

"I can tell you're wanting to tell me something Lizzy, what is it?" she asked, playing with her straight blonde hair, and tipping her head on the side.

"I won't be at this school much longer" I said, after taking a deep breath.

"What do you mean?" she said. I looked at her face, her light eyebrows were scrunched together above the centre of her eyes, with anxiety. She was still twiddling her hair, like she often does when she gets worried about something. I explained what my mum had said last night, about moving house, and schools. I told her I didn't know why.

"My mum seemed so upset," I explained, "but I don't know whether that's because she wants to stay in London and will miss all her friends, or because my dad will not be around so much as normal. She didn't tell me why that is either. What do you think's going on? Do you think I can speak to my dad and stop it happening to make Mum feel better?" I asked. Isabelle bit her lip in thought.

"Well you can try, but that never seems to work with my parents," she said. We both agreed that was not the best option. She then made a few suggestions as to why we were having to move quickly, but she wasn't sure why either. After looking at a new Instagram page which Isabelle had recently followed, as well as some new bright pink nail varnish I'd got free with a fun magazine, we then had to go back to the classroom for the rest of the day's lessons.

During the afternoon, we kept passing secret notes to each other under the desk, which we sometimes do in the afternoon if we were both thinking about the same thing. Miss Bumford eventually caught us, though, and then read out the note to the whole classroom. It was from Isabelle to me and said 'don't worry we can keep in touch on-line and practice our nail art like that too.' When she read this out, Max laughed out in that horrible way he does, throwing his head back, and opening his smelly mouth wide, making fun of us. It made me so angry, that I nearly shouted at him that he should close his mouth as it could stink the whole class out! I managed to control myself, though, when I saw how annoyed Miss Bumford was with us for not concentrating in the first place.

At the end of the school day, Isabelle gave me a big hug.

"Everything's going to be ok you know," she said. "We can still keep in touch, as people stay in touch with each other even when they live on the other side of the world. In some ways it could make meeting up even more fun!" I looked at her feeling happy she had said this, and cared, but I knew it wasn't quite the same as seeing each other at school every day. Once lessons had finished, I packed my rucksack, and for the first time ever, was not looking forward to going home. I didn't really know what to expect, and wasn't sure I would be able to say the right thing. My biggest worry was my mum, I didn't want to upset her, as seeing her crying also upset me, and sometimes saying or doing the right thing is so hard. It was that strange feeling of not knowing what I would feel on opening that front door.

Chapter 3

Within a few weeks it was time for us to move. Robbie's room always looked such a mess. Having to clear it up, and put everything in boxes, was making him angry (as so many things do). I had been looking for every opportunity to speak to my dad on his own without Mum there so I could find out what was going on. I wanted a full explanation if I was having to leave my friends. I didn't feel it was easy to speak to Mum about the move either, as I didn't want to upset her. My big opportunity came when Mum was out buying the groceries and Dad was looking through some paperwork in the sitting room. Robbie was out playing football with friends. I sat down on the sofa next to him.

"Dad can I ask you something."

"Yes" he said, still reading the paperwork in his hands, rubbing his forehead at the same time and biting his lower lip, as he crunched-up one eye in thought.

"Why are we moving and why did Mum say you're not going to be around so much." I could feel my heartbeat getting faster and I began holding my breath, waiting for his response, not sure if he was even going to answer. He looked at me and I think he could tell I was worried.

"Because of my new job we have to move to a different place," he said. He then paused, took a sip from his coffee cup, like he always does when he's thinking, and continued. "My work means I may need to go away for quite long periods at a time." I asked him what

9

his new job was, as he hadn't told us about that, and asked what he meant by long periods? I was about to ask him why, but he stopped me by putting his finger on my lip and said "I will explain things if you'll listen." I held my breath, as I really wanted to speak.

"We will be moving to Southampton as that will be the base for my job. It may be hard to understand, but although that's the base for my new job, I will have to travel away for long periods of time as I will be boarding ships that travel far in the Merchant Navy," my dad explained. Although I really didn't like the idea of our Dad being away extensively, I thought the 'Merchant Navy' sounded like a very grand job. I asked him if that was like defending our country, and he said 'not quite', but he then said "It may mean I can bring special presents back from faraway places." With that he gave me one of his secret smiles that only I know.

"I think this has upset Mummy quite a lot," I whispered, almost worried she could hear me. My dad nodded, acknowledging this, but at the same time looking as though he knew he was doing the right thing. At that point I heard a key turn in the front door lock, and the crinkling sound of grocery bags as my mum returned home. I kept quiet then. I heard her put the bags down in the kitchen, and her footsteps on the hallway floor as she came around and stuck her head into the living room.

"What have you two been up to?" she said in her jokey manner.

"Nothing", I said, which I find is often the easiest answer.

"I think I'll find out soon" she said looking my dad in the eye. My mum then went to the kitchen, asked me to help her put the shopping away, which I did, and then asked me what we would like for dinner. We both talked about what boys probably like after football games, and came to the conclusion that sausage with mash potatoes would keep everyone happy, along with my favourite frozen peas (well they are easy to cook I suppose).

It didn't take long before dinner, and we were all sat around the table. Robbie had a bit more of a smile on his face, due to enjoying his football game since his side won. My mum then asked him how far he had got with tidying his room and packing- the smile soon disappeared! My dad said later that after dinner, he would take us out to the cinema. I was so happy about this as a film I had so wanted to see was showing. Robert and I argued a bit about which film to watch, but eventually I got my way (well he had been playing football all afternoon and I had helped Mum with the shopping and dinner). It was also fun having some popcorn (as Mum doesn't normally allow this but Dad does), and a fizzy drink. I wanted to make the most of our trip to the cinema, as were moving soon, and I didn't know if the cinemas in Southampton would be any good, or even if they had cinemas!

Chapter 4

It seemed time went so quickly. It was not long before the removals van was pulling into the drive to transfer all our belongings. Mum was fretting that the removals men might scratch the sofa as they were too 'heavy handed.' Robert didn't seem to care, he just gave some of his boxes a kick, as though that would make them move faster. Dad just directed the men where to go, arms waving around. He just wanted to get on with it, as he can be so impatient.

Eventually, after Mum checked the house twice over (possibly 3 or 4 times actually), we set off. I had tried to persuade Mum to let me ride in the removals van so I could sit up high, and maybe get a better view of the road, but that was not allowed. It was so boring sitting in the back of my parent's car. The sound of the constant droning of the car tyres on the motorway surface, and swishing of cars going past eventually made me feel a bit sick.

"Are we ever going to get there?" I asked. Robert gave me that 'are you stupid' look again.

"Southampton's miles away," he said.

"I don't know, do I?" I responded. I noticed as time went on, that the background outside the window was getting greener in colour. There were more and more trees, and fields. It felt slightly more interesting when I then saw some fields with sheep and the odd horse as we drove by too. "Maybe I can ride some horses in Southampton", I said.

"Maybe you can" my mum replied with a smile on her face.

After setting off from a petrol station we had to refuel at, I think I must have fallen asleep, as it didn't seem long before I felt the car pulling up next to a house, our new house in fact. It was a typical modern house, alongside a group of very similar looking houses. There was an old hanging basket hanging by the front door, the flowers in it looked a bit dead and dried out, and I felt it could do with improving, especially as the house next door had some lovely flowers in pots surrounding it, as well as a colourful hanging basket.

As we walked in through the front door, it smelt a little bit stale, perhaps dusty, and perhaps hadn't been lived in for a while. The removals van drew-up too, and the men unloaded everything. As they left, one of them told me that 'it looks like you've got a great new place'. It wasn't until I looked at all the boxes filling the corridors of our new house that I realised we then had the horrible task of unpacking everything!

"Do we have to do it now?" I asked

"No" my mum said. "For now, we'll just use what's in our suitcases and deal with this in the morning."

That evening we managed to find a Chinese takeaway shop, from one of the many unread leaflets that were on the floor by the front door-very useful, I thought. We chose noodles, and chicken chow-main, among some other dishes I can't remember the name of, and after enjoying that meal, set up temporary beds. It didn't take long for all of us to fall asleep, as everyone was so tired.

The next day we really did have the boring job of unpacking, and arranging furniture etc. I was surprised at how quickly we managed to do this, even though my brother was continually moaning. I was just desperate for my little laptop so I could speak to Isabelle on-line. Robert and dad didn't take long to sort out all the internet connections and set up our internet hub, so I forgave Robbie for moaning.

After texting Isabelle first, we managed to start chatting quickly after lunch.

"What do you think?" she asked.

"Well it certainly seems more like the countryside" I said, but I was quick to tell her about the possibility of riding horses, and that I'd noticed it seemed to be warmer in Southampton.

"Can you see the sea?" Isabelle asked. I didn't even know we were near the seaside really, but I couldn't see it anyway. If you listened carefully you could sometimes hear a seagull, though, which was nice. I told her about my new bedroom, and we talked about what posters to put up, and colours to make it special. It was beginning to seem a little more exciting than I had originally thought, although I was quite anxious about what my new school would be like. "Don't worry", Isabelle said, like she always does with a big smile. "You'll soon make new friends and I'll always be here for you too, we can chat and text". I told her how it seemed like it was greener with more trees and fields, and she said "that means you can go on some nice walks. I've done that before when we had a short holiday near there."

I wasn't really used to going on many proper walks, or walking holidays as such, but it sounded like something that could be nice. After we finished our conversation and catch-up, I went to join the rest of my family. I didn't tell them about my chat with Isabelle, as I liked to keep that secret, but I mentioned to them the idea of going on nice walks.

"There are lots of those around here" my dad said. "You have The New Forest or even Southampton Common nearby and that has some magical places."

"Maybe we should find out where that is?" I said.

"As well as where you're school is," my dad responded in a slightly deeper tone, dropping his head and looking up, to emphasise the importance.

After that, he suggested that we should go for a short drive to show me where the school was. He also wanted to point out Southampton Common. By car, the school was actually close to the common, and seemed absolutely massive! It was a long white building with the usual wire netting around it, but there were large green fields in front of it, as well as some tennis courts. My first thoughts were that I was scared I could get lost easily. As we drove on, my dad pointed out where The Common was. It was hard to see into the common properly, as there were lots of trees at the boundary with walls that surrounded it. I could see that to get in, you needed to walk down roads which took you in, but did not look designed for a car to travel down. The wall surrounding it seemed to go on such a long distance, it was obvious the common was massive too. I found myself wondering would I get lost in this place? My dad looked at me.

"All new places seem big when you don't know them," he said as if he could read my mind. It was supposed to make me feel better, but I'm not sure it did, as he always seemed to find his way around anywhere!

"Do you like the look of the school?" My mum asked me as we entered through the front door, on coming home.

"We've only just got back!" I said, "It looks big". My mum laughed a little, and got on with sorting out dinner.

"Well I've sorted out your new uniform, it's on your bed", she shouted out from the kitchen. I went up to my bedroom and looked at it. It didn't look that much different from my old summer uniform, but I didn't really like the new colour (green and white), or the fact it was a pinafore dress with a silly white collar. My mum must have bought this without telling me, before we moved. Sometimes you can make problems with colour like that better, though, by painting you nails a nicer colour, or putting a colourful scrunchie and hairclip in your hair. That night, before I went to bed, I painted my nails a fun sparkly purple colour, then found my favourite pink scrunchie and put it out ready for the next day, next to my hairbrush. I felt this could somehow help me look better for my first day at this new school, even though I wouldn't know anyone, which I was dreading a bit. I already felt myself missing Isabelle, my best friend.

-manicure-

Chapter 5

The next day we set off for our new school, St Beckets. I had been thinking about what it would be like so much overnight, that it was hard to sleep. Because of this, I was now feeling a bit tired. It was a sunny day, which was nice, but I didn't know whether my new school would be nice, so the sun didn't make me smile as much as usual. I remember the mass of people rushing around to their classrooms as they were being dropped off, locker doors smashing closed, as people declared their stuff was safely in their little box that no-one else had rights to. I followed the long corridor along to classroom 4, which is where I was told to head, and entered in, seeing a number of other faces, people already sitting at their desks. I just sat anywhere, since I didn't know anyone, so it didn't matter. The girl on my right side smiled, and the boy on my left didn't even seem to notice me. Before I could think any more about it, the teacher walked into the room.

"Good morning class" she said.

"Good morning Mrs Crane," everyone responded. She then told us all that I was a newcomer to the class, which was slightly embarrassing, but we soon got on with our Geography lesson, so it didn't worry me too much.

At break time, the girl sitting next to me said hello, and told me her name was Clare. She seemed quite nice, which made me feel less nervous, and as time went on, she told me a little piece of information about everyone in the classroom.

"The guy sitting on your left is called George, he doesn't say very much and is quite boring," she said.

"Is he horrible?" I asked.

"Well not really, but he's not much fun to chat to." I looked again at his haircut that looked like someone had stuck a bowl on his brown head of hair, then cut around it. I felt a little sorry for him, as it looked just silly. I found it quite funny how she described the twins sitting behind us, who really did look like they were exactly the same with their ginger hair in bunches, and seemed to like playing tricks on people to see if they noticed. I didn't like the sound of the girl called Jane, who Clare said could often 'tell on you' to the teacher.

As the day went on, I gradually began to feel that maybe the school wasn't so scary, and it did not seem long until it was time to go home. I also found myself looking forward to the next day, as we would be playing netball. When I got home, after dinner I called Isabelle, told her about the new school and the people I had met there. She said things had been ok with her, and that she had met a new girl that day who seemed quite nice. She was soon quick to tell me that it didn't affect our friendship, though. As she said that, she held her hands up to the camera on the computer screen, with her fingers posed in the heart shape sign we often show to each other. I explained to her that things felt quite strange, as I was only just starting at the new school, but it would be summer holidays soon. "I suppose so, but it doesn't matter where you are, or how long you've spent there, holidays are brill!" Isabelle said, showing a thumbs up, and a big smile.

As the evening went on, my Dad explained that he would be starting his new job in the next few days. He then looked at both Robert and I with a serious look.

"Now you need to understand that will mean I will be away for a number of months at a time."

"Do you know how long?" I asked.

"Not entirely", he responded, "but it could be two to three, maybe even four months at a time." I tried not to show it, but I could tell he'd noticed the disappointment in my eyes. "Try not to be sad," he said. "Remember, there is so much to discover in Southampton. This weekend we will spend some time looking at some places to visit and walk, as it will be the last weekend before I have to go away." As he said this, I looked at my mum as I knew it had made her sad, but although she didn't smile, she didn't seem quite as upset as before we left our old house. It was as though she had come to terms with everything a little.

As the week went by, I got to know Mrs Crane more. I found her slightly more fun than Miss Bumford. She had quite a high voice, that some people liked making fun of, and light brown hair that was cut in a short bob. Her fringe was swept across her forehead and every so often, she swished her hand across to put it back into place. She asked me how I was getting on with Southampton, and St Becket's. She also said I was doing well (I think she was just being nice as I had only just started at the school). Mrs Crane taught us Geography and History, which I was finding more interesting than it was usually, and Clare seemed to like these subjects too.

Everything was quite unusual for Robbie and I, as we were starting a new school when the summer holidays were soon to start as well. The rest of the term (which only had one week left) seemed to go by very quickly, as each day was so busy with work to do, and things to learn. Before long it was the 'end of term'. On the last day, just before the last lesson, I asked Clare, my new friend, if she felt she would be able to meet-up at some point in the summer holidays. At first I wasn't sure what she would say, as it seemed like we'd only just met. She said that would be a nice idea, and we exchanged mobile numbers for WhatsApp and Instagram to stay in touch with each other. I hoped she would like my profile pictures which I didn't think were so bad (even though I'm not very good at taking pictures of myself).

At the weekend, my dad asked my mum to prepare a picnic basket of food with a rug, and then loaded it up into the back of the car. He drove us up to the Southampton Common Area (which he had previously pointed out to me) and parked. We all got out, and he gradually began describing the area as he pointed with his finger in various directions. Looking at his face, I could see he felt this to be a special area, full of nice sites and sounds. He stated that this was 'The Common', but it could be accessed if you were walking up to it, through the old graveyard. He pointed towards the graveyard, which just seemed so far back with stone walls around it. I could just about see old church-like buildings somewhere back in that area. I could also see a gateway that would take you between The Common and graveyard. Part of me felt a little scared of it, as I wondered if you might see ghosts in a graveyard, but tried not to think about that as there were so many other lovely things to see and we were a long way away. Many people were walking about, chatting, walking dogs, prams and elderly relatives. We could see that other people were setting out picnic mats, with some throwing frisbees and sticks or balls for fun. Some people were even throwing breadcrumbs out to swans and ducks you could see on a lovely lake there too. It was not so pristine as the parks in London often looked, and it seemed as if nature was allowed to grow it's own way a little bit more.

My mum looked at us with a big smile, rolled out a picnic mat onto the grass. She opened the big bag full of food. The mat felt lovely and warm as I jumped onto it. My mum then got out some sausage rolls, her smile getting bigger, holding them up. A small dog came up behind her, sniffing at them. This made her laugh. The dog's owner apologised and quickly hurried him on. We all enjoyed some nice fizzy drinks and I loved my cheese and pickle sandwiches (which were nicer for me than smelly sausage rolls). My dad then looked around, bringing his hand up to his chin, and said "and I want you all to know that I love you all very much". He frowned a little and then said "This is a special place to me as I enjoyed it as a child and you can now all enjoy it. Because I'm going away for a while doesn't mean I don't think about you". He then went on to say "it actually means I will think about you even more". I could tell my mum looked slightly sad. My dad then gave my mum a big kiss on her cheek, and said "and your mum makes the best sandwiches ever so maybe you can persuade her to take you on more picnics."

"Well, that's more likely if you two help me prepare the food bag!" my mum responded quickly, looking at Robbie and myself.

Once we'd finished enjoying all the food and fizzy drinks, we played chase, had a good look at the lovely animals, such as the swans and squirrels that loved to dart up the many trees. We fed the ducks a bit with left over bits from sandwiches (even though there was a sign that said we shouldn't) as well. I noticed a Robin (which I had only seen on television before) and got a great picture of it with my phone, singing. We then went home that evening feeling a bit tired after burning up lots of energy. As I lay on my bed, I felt a little bit down as something reminded me that our dad would be leaving in the morning. I cheered myself up by posting a picture of the singing Robin on 'Facebook' and it immediately got a thumbs-up from Isabelle, and a few other friends from my old school. With that, I went to sleep after hiding my laptop under the bed so my brother didn't borrow it!

Chapter 6

The next morning my mum cooked a fried breakfast with poached eggs to make sure my dad had a nice 'breakfast memory'. Once we'd all finished eating, he packed his case into the back of his car and gave us all a big hug. I felt some tears welling up in my eyes, and tried really hard not to let them spill over my cheeks. Eventually I couldn't help it though, and as we waved at the car driving away, I just burst into tears. My mum put her arms around me.

"Don't worry, we can still speak to him and the time will be gone before you know it," she said. I gave her a forced smile to try and cheer her up too, but it felt different in the house, almost like something had sucked a feeling from inside out, almost like an energy hole missing.

I looked at my brother, and wasn't quite sure what to do with myself. He gave me a look as if to say 'Stop being so pathetic', and then went off to his room to play some computer games. At first I thought I should speak to Isabelle, but then I thought I needed to get to know where to go in this new town a bit better, so instead I sent a text to Clare to see if she wanted to go for a walk with me. I was surprised at how quickly she replied. She said she was quite busy helping her mum and grandmother making a cake today, but could go for a walk tomorrow. I immediately texted back as that was great, and added a picture of a cake at the end of the text for fun. It made me feel like I wanted to make one too. I asked my mum if we could, but she said the mixer was still packed away in a box, and we didn't have enough flour. I felt a bit disappointed, but watched some little blogs on 'Youtube' about how to make a fun one, as I wasn't really sure how to properly!

The next day, I met up with Clare, who actually lived close to us, and she suggested we take a walk in 'The Common'. I said that sounded great, and mentioned how my dad had taken us there for a picnic, but I didn't really know it or how to get through it, as it was such a large place. My mum agreed to let me go, but asked that we were careful near the road. We walked up the pavement beside the main road towards it, and Clare led me down a car-free lane. Gradually I could see how there were many trees around, and large expanses of grass ahead. She then said we should go through the 'old cemetery' to take us through to the common. As we walked through, we moved past two old churches (that looked as though they were never visited). We then went through the old cemetery, it also felt as though it was a very neglected place. Many stones were at funny angles or broken. Some graves almost looked as though they'd been deliberately smashed-up, and it would have been almost impossible to know who was buried there. Some raised areas looked like they may have had a gravestone there once, but it had been lost. Lots of high weeds, grasses and brambles grew over the ground and graves, along with different coloured moss that had spread over stones. Some plants had grown so large, but almost grand in a unique way as they'd been left to grow how they wanted, and now displayed many flowers or colourful leaves to a great towering height. Clare looked at me and giggled.

"You shouldn't look so scared," she said.

"I've never been in a graveyard before," I told her. "It feels so big and it's strange to think there are dead people underneath us." Clare Led me forward through the cemetery down a central straight path.

"Well let's get through to The Common, it's much less scary," she responded.

As we walked through, I could then see an open gate at the end of the path, and there were people walking past. Once we passed through the gate, Clare threw open her arms.

"And this is Southampton Common," she said. I looked all around me and there were on-going green fields, with pathways surrounding them. In the distance I could see a lake with birds flying around. Every so often someone would jog by, either listening to music, or chatting while puffing on their mobile phone. I then saw a young mum jogging while pushing a pram, and there were quite a few people walking their dog (or more than one dog).

"I would love to have a dog," I said to Clare.

"I love dogs too", she said. "My mum and dad said we don't have the space or time for one, but I'd let it sleep in my room, and I would give it secret time." We both laughed, and carried on walking around. As we walked, I saw many different types of trees, sections of woods, water in lakes and streams, even a playground at one point, and so much grass-filled fields with buttercups. It was a massive place. I also saw that in one area there were a few patches of burnt grass in square shapes "Oh, that's where people have had a barbeque," Clare said.

"I'd be a bit scared to light a fire out here" I said.

"I think I would too" Clare replied. We carried on walking around and completed a loop to take us back to where we started. Although we had been on a long walk, I could see that there were so many areas that could still be explored, and walked through, as the common went on for miles.

After our trip, we walked home, and made a cup of tea at my house. We then agreed to meet up again to go on some more similar walks. Secretly I couldn't wait, as I could tell Clare was really nice, and I could sense we might be able to have an enjoyable time, especially since she knew the place well.

That evening I spoke to Isabelle on-line, and told her about the new places I had seen.

"I felt so sad when our dad left, but going for that walk with Clare helped prevent me from feeling so upset", I said.

"It sounds fun" said Isabelle. I quickly told her that she was still my best friend, in case she felt Clare had taken that place, and also described how scary the old cemetery was. "Cemeteries' can be interesting and exciting places you know" Isabelle said.

"Really?" I asked.

"Well, I bet if you look carefully at some of the gravestone, the dates on some them were ages ago, maybe even 100 years! Some of the graves have more than one person, and some tell unusual stories!".

"Don't you feel it's a bit odd looking at them?" I asked.

"Well it can tell us something about history" Isabelle responded. "You can sometimes imagine what that person was like 100 years ago, maybe even more. I wonder what kind of clothes they would have worn?".

"Have you ever even been to a cemetery?" I asked.

"Well, once I went to a funeral, and it was for someone I didn't even know, and I got a bit bored when we were standing in the cemetery, so I went to look at the gravestones, and found the really old ones, especially when they had little statues on them, very interesting!".

"I think I'll take your word on that," I said to Isabelle, and we both laughed.   I told her about how the fields were so big, and it would be fun having all that space to run around in, maybe play with a Frisbee, like I'd seen some people playing today. "Perhaps at some point my mum will let you come and stay for a few days" I said.

"I can't wait" Isabelle responded.

Chapter 7

"Mum," I asked, while looking over my cup of tea at breakfast.

"Why am I sensing a 'can I have' coming on?" my mum asked smiling.

"Well it's not quite a can I have" I said, with a sneaky smile.

"Well tell me then," she said.

"Do you think Isabelle can come and stay with us for a little bit?" I asked. My mum looked at me, seemed to think a little.

"If her mum and dad are ok about it, then maybe that'd be possible once we've managed to finish unpacking all the boxes and tidy our home up a bit more," she responded. I felt really pleased as I was in part expecting my mum to say no, as we'd only just moved in.

After breakfast, I got to work unpacking everything and putting belongings away. In my bedroom it didn't take too long, and I managed to put up a few posters I had stored. Some of the posters were quite old, so I thought about how it could be fun getting some new posters, and kept that at the back of my mind so I could persuade my mum when we next went shopping, and also have a look on-line for fun ideas, so I could even make my own.

In the afternoon, I asked my mum if we could go for a walk, as I wanted to get to know the common better, and to take lots of pictures. I felt maybe these could be put up in my new bedroom. She agreed, and we walked up towards the common together. I showed her how you could walk into it via the graveyard, and felt happy that she was with me, as the thought of dead bodies scared me. As we walked through, my mum looked at me.

"See, there aren't any ghosts," she said. She started looking closely at the gravestones and seemed very interested in the place, which helped me feel that it was perhaps generally a very interesting place too. We walked together to an old display board, and she pointed out little posters behind the glass. One poster mentioned occasional tours of the place, and also displayed information about some of the people buried there and 'the friends of the old graveyard'. "These are people who work for charity to try and keep the place alive if you can call it that," she explained. As she spoke, I looked around and saw how abandoned it looked, but the way nature had taken over and how most of the graves looked a mess was perhaps a bit sad as the names of some peoples' graves were really lost forever. It was odd, though, how in some places, the occasional narrow pathway had been strimmed out. It meant you could walk to some graves that had some flowers on them, and these were perhaps visited every so often by someone.

I also read some interesting information on one of the first graves you saw as you entered, and how the person buried had been struck by lightening which had killed them about 100 years ago, when they were only 18 years old. It was a slightly scary place, but there really were so many unusual things to see. The information on other stones, the beautiful flowers and bushes, that must have just appeared there placed by the force of nature. Although it was a place for the dead, it felt very much alive as every so often people would walk through past us from The Common with a smile or a nod to acknowledge our presence, which you certainly didn't get from strangers on a London street.

My mum and I completed a small walk and went home with me feeling like I would like to spend more time looking through The Old Graveyard and The Common. When I got home, I sent a text to Clare and asked if through the holidays we could go for some walks through those places to take some pictures and get to know the place a bit better. She quickly responded saying she'd love to, and with a bit of coaxing, I managed to persuade my mum to say yes (well it was for my education I said). Clare suggested we should meet the next day. That night I lay in bed thinking about pictures I could take, which I could send to Isabelle, to show her what the area was like. I also spent a bit of time listening to some of my favourite music before falling asleep with the earphones still in!

Chapter 8

The next day I met Clare outside the entrance to 'The Old Graveyard'. We walked through it together and she pointed out a few unusual graves. Some graves held young people, even babies. Some showed signs that people from the military were buried as well. One thing I noticed, was that some of the graves had strange blue wooden stakes pushed into the ground at the end of them. The pegs looked like they had been there a long time, as the paint was chipped on some, and peeling off. It was odd, as it seemed like something connected these 'blue staked' graves with each other. I asked Clare if she knew what these blue stakes showed or meant, but she wasn't sure. She said she hadn't really thought about it before. We noted, though, that the graves they were in were particularly old, with very overgrown grass, weeds, and moss. It was hard to tell the names of people buried in them. There were a few graves that seemed better kept, with fresh flowers on, and fresher stones, but none of these had blue stakes.

As we came out of the graveyard, Clare got out a frisbee, and we played with this for some time around the common, running around the large grassland. At one point, it was caught by an old lady, with long white hair. She gave a big smile, and threw it back to us. It was almost caught by a dog on one occasion, but Clare just about managed to grab it in time. I so enjoyed the game. Although in some way it seemed like quite an old-fashioned thing to do, it was so fun, running about, in all that space.

After playing around, we decided to walk around The Common, and treated ourselves to an ice-cream from a stall there. I kept this all secret from my mum when we got home. I did tell her, though, about how fun our frisbee game was, and how a dog almost caught it before us. My mum commented how funny dogs can be, and carried on making dinner.

Bedtime seemed to come very quickly, and I slept well that night. It was almost as if a lot of the things I was worrying about had calmed down in my head. The house was also looking quite a bit tidier, and in a strange way, it was beginning to feel like home. Before going to sleep I thought I'd go on to facebook to show some of the pictures of birds and flowers I had taken. Isabelle clicked that she 'liked them' with a thumbs up. I then texted Clare to see if she wanted to meet the following day for a similar walk or game. She agreed and we then decided a time and place to meet. I felt slightly excited as at the end of the text she mentioned that she had some fun things to tell me, I had no idea what?

Chapter 9

I stood at the top of the road that led towards the Common, the next morning. I was waiting for Clare at what had become our almost daily meeting place. It was becoming normal now for us to walk through the old graveyard, and I recognised the odd person's face as it seemed a few people walked through there regularly. I could still not believe how overgrown the whole area was, though. Thick clumps of brambles grew across many areas, with lots of tall grass, and sprouting baby trees. There were massive rhodedendrum bushes with pink flowers galore, and various large thick fern trees that were impinging on the walkway. It was almost as if a number of these large trees were randomly placed there, like the sprouting ones, but had now grown to be, in some cases, huge, getting bigger each time we came. I looked at how many graves were so overgrown that all that could be seen was a tiny bit of broken stone poking through the brambles, some just like soil lumps, but some stones still stood there proudly, even if at an angle. The way some birds, perched for long periods of time on the top of a few of them was also fun to watch, as they didn't care what they perched on.

As we walked along the pathway, various wildlife could be seen, more than I had ever seen before in London. Pigeons were plentiful, balanced on gravestones and various strange statues, but occasionally a squirrel could be seen darting around, with a nut in its mouth. I asked Clare about what she had wanted to tell me, that she mentioned last night. She said she was so happy, as her dad had bought a new camera for her as an early birthday present. She proudly showed it to me, and got out the cool pink neck strap, so she could walk around with it hanging around her neck. I loved it, and was a little bit jealous, but at the same time pleased for her. It was an unusual square shape, and pink colour, and not everyone would realise it was a camera, but it looked so fun! Clare said we could make up a scrap book of photos, particularly of the wildlife in the park, as the camera could also print pictures out. I was pleased, as this sounded fun, and in some ways, we had already started this on our phones, but a proper camera was that bit more special.

"What's most fun about taking pictures is capturing pictures that are hard to get, like animals that move quickly", she said. I agreed.

"Maybe we should walk further into the graveyard (away from the main path) so that it's more likely we can get the best shots", I said. She agreed, so we started to take the smaller, almost invisible paths to get more deeply into the graveyard and undergrowth.

As we moved forward, I could see how it went on much further than it first seemed.

"Look there," Clare said. As I looked, I could see the top of a small ginger headed animal peeking out from behind the long grass on what must have been a grave. "Quickly, let's try and get a picture". As we moved forward, unfortunately it scared the animal, and I was not sure what it was. Then it jumped up and out from behind the grass and ran. We could then see it was a small dog. Clare and I chased after it, but were not fast enough to get a picture. A ginger tail could just about be seen disappearing under the grass as the dog ran off. We looked out for it for a short while, but then decided to carry on. We managed to get a lovely picture of a squirrel, and a few unusual birds I hadn't seen before, and then carried on into the main Common. After playing a few games, we had a quick look through some of our images, and saved the ones we liked best. I told her about the problem of my room posters looking a bit old, and she suggested we might be able to put together some new exciting posters of our pictures. I then realised just how fun taking some pictures can really be!

Once I got home, I thought more about our day that seemed to go by so quickly, as it was now time for dinner. My mum put together some spaghetti bolognaise, which my brother moaned about, after which he went to play computer games, as usual. I sat and watched the TV with my mum for a while, who was definitely now less stressed than when we first arrived. I later went up to my room. As I lay on my bed, I thought about what we had seen and done that day. I wondered whether the dog we'd seen had just strayed from it's owner a little, whether it was lost or if it just lived on its own in the graveyard. I didn't really know, but I hoped it was ok. Although I told myself not to worry too much about it, as I lay in bed going to sleep, it was still at the back of my mind as I drifted off to sleep.

Chapter 10

It was soon the weekend. My dad called, and I was so happy to hear his voice on the phone. He had a long chat with my brother, who, although normally thinks adults are not worth talking to, seemed to enjoy his chat. I told my dad about the new school, and how we'd also managed to unpack most things. I also told him about my new friend. He reminded me not to forget about Isabelle, and also asked what activities we'd got up to.

Our conversation then went on to the Common, the Old Graveyard, and the wildlife. We discussed Clare's wonderful camera, and I even told him what shape and colour it was (to try and hint about what birthday present I might like). He asked what pictures we had taken? I explained pictures of wild animals and even close-ups of some wild-flowers which were great to capture too. He agreed with me. I then told him about the small dog we had seen, that disappeared. He commented that it sounded like a stray dog, and that if we saw it again, we should maybe tell someone. There was just so much to tell him, that it was hard to stop talking.

That weekend, I also had a long on-line chat with Isabelle, and she showed me some of the new stickers she had got. Some of them were really lovely, and were now stuck in pride of place on her old laptop. I told her how much I missed her.

"Well I'm saving some of my best stickers for a swap when we see each other" she said. I told her I couldn't wait.

On Sunday, we did the boring food shopping, which always takes so long, but I did manage to persuade my mum to buy some chocolate spread, which is not always easy. She also bought me a page of fun stickers, which was unusual. I kept looking at the central sticker in the small collection, as it was of a girl holding a little dog up to her face, quite cute. I pointed to it, and told my mum how it was different.

"That's a chihuahua dog," my mum said pinching my cheek. When we got home, and finished putting the shopping away, I stuck it onto the first page of my notebook, right in the centre. I then took a picture of it, and sent a text of the picture to Clare. She sent me a thumbs-up picture back, which made me smile. Her text also asked if I wanted to go for walk the following day and take some more pictures. We then arranged a time to meet at the usual place.

Before I went to bed that evening, I thought a little bit more about what my dad had said. If the dog was stray, how do you report it? Who do you report it to? What would they do with a stray dog? Would they put it down, or in horrible kennels? The more I thought about it, the more worried it made me. I then thought I'd discuss it with Clare in the morning, as she might know what to do.

Chapter 11

"Hi" I shouted, as I saw Clare waving her arm at me from our usual meeting place.

"I can't wait to show you some of the pictures I've printed," she said, as I jogged up to her. From her rucksack, she pulled out a picture of a robin singing from an oak branch. It was a magnified picture, almost 3D, so you could see its little eyes and red breast more clearly than I thought possible.

"That looks brilliant" I said, "Lets see what we can get today."

We walked on, and didn't have any planned route, but just moved wherever we thought we could get a good picture. As we advanced further into the graveyard, and under a giant redwood tree, it was becoming harder to walk straight through, and we had to concentrate hard on which direction to walk to make it through the undergrowth, often getting prickled by the thorns. I got out my phone, and managed to take a picture of a pigeon, which I was proud of, even though it was perhaps not as interesting as the pretty colourful butterfly Clare took a picture of. I was determined to get a picture of another butterfly or even a squirrel, so encouraged us to move on.

As we got even deeper in, the little ginger head of the doggy we had seen yesterday, bobbed his head above the long grass on one grave.

Both of us froze, as we tried not to scare it. Clare quickly took a picture, and then reached her hand out so the dog could sniff it. He tentatively sniffed her knuckles, and then rushed out. In some way, this little doggy seemed slightly less scared. Clare noted that he didn't have a collar on, and she seemed worried about this. He (if it was a he) didn't seem unwell, though.

"What do you think we should do?" I asked.

"Well I suppose we could ask the RSPCA, or the blue cross, or even the Dogs Trust, they might know" Clare suggested.

Both of us sat down, got out our iphones, and searched on-line through the RSPCA website, and I managed to find some information on the Dogs Trust website. It mentioned that we should not call them unless we thought the dog was abused or unwell. It did say we should contact the dog warden for our council, and the nearest vets, or consider putting out posters to advertise this dog has been found. Clare managed to take a good picture of this doggie, and felt we could walk to a vets she knew that was nearby. I searched on the council's website and managed to find a number to call. We let their dog warden know all about the dog, and where we had found it. The dog warden told me her name was Charlotte, and she said she would come and track the dog down, and possibly take it to a dog rescue centre. She said she could let us know which one, and that she was impressed with us for contacting her. I asked if anyone had reported a similar dog lost, and she said no-one had.

As Clare and I stood up, the dog ran away, and we were unable to catch up with it. I was a bit worried, but Clare said stray dogs like this usually stay around the same sort of place. She took a picture of where we were, and we continued our walk. After later circling the Common, Clare then showed me where the vets was. It was actually in a house converted into a veterinary surgery just behind the house I was living! We went in and asked the receptionist if we could talk to the vet about a stray dog. She went away, and then came back, saying that he would be out to talk in 10 minutes time.

When he came out, the vet introduced himself as Dr Tolburt, and then gave a big smile, as he wiped the line of brown hair away from his eyes. He directed us to two seats in the empty waiting room.

"How can we help you then?" He said

"I'm really worried about a doggie we found" I replied. Clare then went on to explain all about the small ginger fluffy dog we had seen in the old graveyard. She also mentioned we had told the council dog warden, but thought he might know the area better.

"Oh yes", he said. "I sometimes take my dog for a walk there". He then went on to explain that he would have a look this evening, and if he found it, he would check if the dog was microchipped. If not, he would take it to the nearest dog rescue centre. Dr Tolburt promised he would let us know the result of his search. He then took our phone numbers, gave us a smile and said he needed to get on with his clinic.

That evening, I couldn't stop thinking about that little doggie. I looked again at the picture Clare had sent to me of his face. We had both agreed we thought the dog was 'a he,' but could not be sure, so just agreed we would call it a 'he'. His eyes were so cute, human, almost baby-like. His hair was quite dishevelled. I decided to call him 'Scruffy,' as his fluffy hair was at so many angles, my mum would have called it Scruffy. I hadn't really told her much about him yet, but thought I may have to soon. As I fell asleep, I really hoped that there would be a text on my phone in the morning from the vet, and fell asleep with the phone next to my face.

Chapter 12

I checked my phone as soon as I woke up at 7am. I felt so disappointed, as there were no new texts. After having a shower, I went downstairs, and sat at our kitchen table, while my mum put some slices of bread into the toaster.

"Your look pretty miserable," my brother said, as he walked into the room. He moved towards the toaster, and grabbed the toast out as it popped out.

"Hey! That was mine!" I said.

"Well now it's mine as you're too slow", he responded and gave me a cheeky smile, then leaving for football practice. In some ways, I didn't really care, as my mind was on other things.

"I'll put some more in for you", my mum said, giving me a wink. She seemed in a good mood today, unlike me. As she made us both some tea, I spread some butter and honey on the toast. I then put my mobile next to the plate. "You seem to be staring at that rather a lot today", my mum said. Almost as if it could hear what I was thinking, it rang. I answered it straight away.

"Has he called you?" I heard Clare's voice say.

"No," I responded. "I'll give you a call or text as soon as I hear anything" I said. I carried on having my breakfast as my mum read the paper, every so often lifting an eye above it to see what I was doing with my mobile.

"You seem to be using that thing rather a lot lately," she said. I kept quiet, for the moment.

Just after I finished washing up my cup and plate, the phone rang. I quickly took off the rubber gloves, and rushed over to it.

"Hello, it's Dr Tolburt."

"Hello" I responded. The vet then went on to tell me that he had found the dog, and it did not have a microchip, so he had taken it to our nearest dog rescue centre which was not very far from us. I quickly took a pen to write down the name of the rescue centre, and the address.

"I have informed the council's dog warden, as well in case he belongs to someone," he said.

"We had done that too", I replied. Dr Tolburt said he was pleased, and that Charlotte the dog warden had mentioned she was impressed with us too.

"Well I love animals", I said, perhaps without really realising this, and that I had an audience.

"Well, you can come to the practice if you like and spend a little time getting to know what vets do if you like". I felt myself smiling, and said I would love to sometime perhaps. After that, our conversation ended. I looked down at the page I had written on, digesting our conversation, and realising that I would have to call the rescue centre if we wanted to see that lovely little bouncy doggie again.

"So, what was that all about?" my mum asked. At first I wasn't sure whether to tell her, or not. I then thought, that because she was in a good mood, I should take the opportunity!

"Mum," I said.

"Yes," she said in a slow way, as if she was expecting to hear a request for something. From then on, I explained to her about the dog, and that it was now in a rescue centre, and about the vets and what our phone-call had been about.

"Do you think we can visit the dog?" I asked, almost expecting her to say no.

"Well, I suppose it wouldn't harm, as long as you don't get any funny ideas," she said. I also told her about how the vets said I could spend some time with him in the clinic, and surprisingly she didn't seem too worried about that either!

After my mum and I finished chatting, I sent a text to Clare, asking her to meet me for a catch-up. We met near the playground, and I got out the piece of paper with the dog rescue centre's address on it. Clare was also keen to go there to see the dog, but didn't feel her parents would take us. We looked at whether we could travel by bus on Clare's public transport phone application, but it wasn't easy. In the end we realised we'd have to ask my mum. Later we had a fun run around playing with our frisbee, which was becoming a regular thing. I then went home and asked Mum if she would take both of us to the rescue centre. She took a deep breath in, made a 'hmmmm' sound, as she screwed her mouth up to one side, and then she said she would! She contacted the centre to ask if we could just see the dog, and I immediately texted Clare. We sorted out a good time in the morning to meet , as my mum agreed to take us both. I checked the opening times, and later that night couldn't stop thinking about what it would be like there.

Chapter 13

Clare jumped into the back of our car with me the next day, as we picked her up on the way to the rescue centre.

"I can't wait", I said.

"Do you think we should let Dr Tolburt know?" she asked.

"Maybe we should tell him how the doggie is when we get back", I said. It didn't actually take very long to get there, and after we got out of the car, I almost ran to the main entrance. We went over to the receptionist and asked if we could see the dog I had already named 'Scruffy'. As I said this, Clare showed a picture of him to the lady. She seemed to immediately recognise him from the picture,

"Ahh, he's a special one", she said, pushing her thick blonde hair behind her ears. It wasn't quite long enough at the front to fit into her head band that was a lovely orange colour. "Were you interested in adopting him?"

"We just wanted to see him," I said, before my mum jumped in with a 'no'.

The lady took us round to the back kennels and pointed him out. Clare and I crouched down, looking at the ginger ball of fluff looking up at us from behind the bars.

"It seems so horrible seeing him in a cage" I heard my mum say, to my surprise. The lady let us walk him round in a small patch of grass used to exercise the dogs on a lead.

"He's so lovely", Clare said.

"I can't believe he's been on his own in the park without a home," I responded. We spent some time stroking him, and found he had become slightly less scared of people, although still quite anxious. I was allowed to give him a small treat, and he seemed to be warming more to me, in fact my heart was melting, as his cute baby-like eyes looked up at my face. Just as I was thinking how much affection I had for him, the lady came around and told us he needed to go back to his kennel now.

As we were leaving, I noticed my mum talking to the receptionist while I walked with Clare, although I wasn't sure what she was saying. We got into the car, and as we were driving away, I wondered if I could find a way to the see that little dog again. I asked my mum if that was possible, and she didn't say yes or no, but I got quite a positive feeling from her reaction and perhaps a secret smile?

That evening I spoke to my old friend Isabelle, and told her about the dog. I asked her what she thought. She said she wished she could see him. I held up the picture of him, which she loved. She then asked if she thought there could be any chance I could travel to London so we could have a proper girly hug.

"How about the weekend?" I asked.

The next morning, I asked mum about travelling to London to see Isabel.

"Ooh, I'm not sure about you travelling on the train on your own," she said. My mum seemed to think for a while, then said she knew some people who might be taking the train then. Amazingly, she phoned one who she found really was travelling there, and agreed to travel with me. I was so happy, it seemed ages since I had seen my old friend!

For the rest of the week, Isabelle and I were texting all kinds of fun ideas we could get up to that weekend. It seemed to take forever until Friday evening finally arrived. My mum's friend Susanne eventually came very smartly dressed, and was really fun to talk to on the journey up to London. Once we arrived at the station, she then took me on the tube to Isabelle's house, which was a relief, as the thought of travelling on the underground was a very scary thought. When Isabelle opened the door, her big smile and scrunched-up eyes made me feel so happy as she threw her arms around me. After we thanked her, Susanne gave me a quick hug, then left to get to the theatre. As she left, Isabelle grabbed my hand, pulled me into the house, and then up the stairs to her bedroom.

She jumped on her bed with a scream, and pulled me on. While we sat with cross-legs, her black cat, which was curled up in the corner of her room jumped on as well. Isabelle stroked it on the head, then pulled it into her lap, as it purred.

"I can't believe you're here", she said.

"Neither can I", I responded. "I've missed you so much!" As I chatted about my new school, what Southampton was like, as well as what Clare and I had been doing, Isabelle put a finger to my mouth. She then asked me to tell her all about the dog I had secretly named Scruffy. I told her how we had found him, and how the vet had helped us get Scruffy to the dog centre.

"I do find it sad, though, when you see them locked in a cage," Isabel said.

"Well, I suppose so, but at least he gets fed, and they seem to like him there," I said.

"Have you visited him yet?" Isabelle asked. I told her we had, and that he was so lovely. "Do you think you'd like a four-legged friend?" Isabelle asked with a cheeky look in her eye, like she often has. She held Morris the cat up to her face as she said this with a grin.

"Well, I don't think my mum would let us anyway," I said. "I suppose it would be a nice dream." "He's just so sweet."

"You shouldn't take looking after a dog lightly I suppose. Dog's aren't just for Christmas, but they can be very special friends," Isabelle reminded me.

That evening we had a nice meal, and talked about what we could do the next day. We both wanted to go to the cinema, and Isabelle's mum agreed to take us. We later spent some time pumping up a blow-up bed for me to sleep on, and put some fresh sheets down on it. I wasn't sure we were going to manage to sleep that night, but after chatting for a while in the dark, it didn't seem to take long before we both fell asleep on it. We were then waking up to the new morning, with a curled-up Morris at the end of the bed.

As we sat in the kitchen after washing and getting dressed, Isabelle grabbed her favourite cereal box from the cupboard, and asked me if I wanted coco-pops too. I didn't really feel like that, and made some toast instead. As I bit into the crispy piece of toast, we both looked at the latest films to see. Isabel's mum then took us to the cinema, as she had promised.

I enjoyed that day so much, even though I wasn't really concentrating on the film, just because I was sitting next to my old friend. It was a cartoon picture film, with fun characters, along with a few magical charms. Some of the songs were also nice to listen to, perhaps even hum along to without realising. When we got home, Isabelle got out some cardboard, pens and coloured clay she had to try and make a similar charm to the one in the film. Once she finished, she held it up.

"And now it needs to go on a necklace, so you can carry around the magical charm," she explained. I laughed, and said I could use an old necklace chain that I had at home so that I could carry it around as a 'best friends necklace.' She was pleased with this response, as I put the handmade charm into my bag, giggling. The funny thing is that even though it perhaps seemed a bit silly, it was also special, as I knew I would not be able to see Isabelle for quite some time after that weekend.

Later we played a few computer games, after looking through pictures we'd both taken, and before we knew it, it was time to go home. My mum had agreed to come and pick me up, and as she knocked on the front door, I felt my heart sink a little. As I left, I thanked Isabelle's mum, and gave my friend a big hug. As I did this, she whispered in my ear.

"Don't forget to try and visit your new four-legged friend and see if he can become your friend forever." As we drove back in the car, I thought about this, and wondered whether it would ever be possible for that to happen. I could almost see his beautiful little face, and thought how nice it would be to stroke his soft fluffy head. I then almost told myself off, as knew that was unlikely to ever happen, so closed my eyes, and let the sound of the motorway grumble on in the background.

As we got closer to home, I heard my mum talking.

"Hey you sleepy head, you know we are nearly home."

"Great", I said. She then looked at me in the driver's rear-view mirror.

"I've got something interesting to tell you soon," she said.

"Is dad coming home?" I asked.

"No, but you'll have to wait and see." From the way my mum said this with her serious expression, I really wasn't sure what to expect. Was is it something to do with my brother? Were we moving again? Oh, I didn't know, but I was now looking forward to getting back to the place I was beginning to feel was our home.

Chapter 14

As the car moved into the driveway, my mum seemed to be smiling. She got out, putting the key into the lock, and ushered us into the house. She then sat us down, pulling me to the seat next to her. She called my brother into the room, then making him sit down. At that point I was getting a little worried, but at the same time excited.

"What is it Mum?" I asked. "Is Dad coming home?" She laughed, and said no. She then took a deep breath, looked at both my brother and then myself, and asked

"How would you two feel about getting a dog?" I couldn't believe what I was hearing.

"Well you know Mum, I'd love it," I responded. She then explained that she expected both of us to be fully involved in properly caring for it, if we got one.

"Do you know what that really means?" She asked. I said I knew I could do it, and would find more information to make sure I cared for it properly. She looked pleased with that statement.

"What dog do you think we could get?" I asked. My mum thought about it a bit, and then admitted that while we weren't looking, she had spoken to the people running the dog shelter, and wondered whether we could look after the dog I'd already mentally named Scruffy.

"I know you've had a difficult time lately," she said to both of us, "and I think we could do with something positive to get us through the summer holidays since your dad won't be around." My mum then explained how we would all need to visit the shelter again, and have a discussion/fill in some forms with the shelter managers, as well as spend a little time there with Scruffy to ensure we were able to look after him. I was so happy, and said we should go as soon as she was happy to.

The following week my mum took my brother and I to the dog shelter, and we discussed with them how to look after the dog I'd named Scruffy, and walked, then played with him for a while. Some long-winded forms were filled in, and soon we were taking home our first ever dog! I kept thinking of all the things the people at the shelter had said about when to feed him, and how often to take him out to the loo. I even watched a few clips on the internet, and the DogsTrust website about what to do when your first dog comes home, but I was still feeling very nervous. What if he weed on the floor? Would my mum then send him back? When we got home, Scruffy was sniffing around everywhere, and at first was reluctant to lie down in the dog bed we'd bought him. I kept taking him outside, in case he needed to go to the loo, and before long I recognised signs that suggested he needed it, like the strange sniffing around the grass, often in circles. That night, Scruffy wined quite a lot, and I wasn't sure what to do. I went and lay downstairs with him for a while, and that seemed to help. In the morning my mum explained that we should expect these sorts of episodes at first as he was getting used to his new home.

Over the next few days, Scruffy settled down, and seemed less anxious. He liked to lie with me on the sofa. My mum said he wasn't allowed on the sofa at first, but she didn't seem to notice when he was lying with me. I started taking him for short walks on the Common, which he enjoyed, and then begun to look for variations in where we walked. I spoke to Clare, and she asked if we could go for walks together across the area, as she knew lots of different routes through The Common. We met the next day, and gradually walked in through a little sideroad. "This road also takes you into the Old Graveyard" Clare said, as we walked on. I looked down at Scruffy, who seemed very happy as he looked up at me. As we walked into the old graveyard, I recognised and remembered the way it looked so abandoned, with lopsided gravestones, many broken, or overgrown, with weeds and foliage. Scruffy seemed quite alert, as though there were things in that undergrowth we didn't know about, but he did. I then remembered how really that was a place he should know well, as we had found him there originally!

Our new doggie seemed to be sniffing at various places with excitement, patches of burial sites, plants and stones.

"Maybe another dog peed up it," Clare said with a giggle.

"Lovely" I responded. I felt it was interesting how there seemed even more foliage than when we had seen it last time, and carried on walking along the path.

"This path will take us through to the main common" Clare said. For the rest of the walk, we moved around the common in a large circle, getting to see the swans and various birds, as well as other dogs with their owners. I felt so proud that I was holding a lead for a dog that was now a member of our family! I even got a few nods from other dog owners, as they walked by with their dogs. I felt almost part of a little club, well, sort of!

At the end of the walk, Clare suggested we should go for walks in the Common together with Scruffy regularly, as she really liked him, and we had the whole summer to enjoy! I agreed, and was pleased as someone who knew the place better would be with us. When we finished our walk, we gave each other a hug, and Clare bent down to Scruffy. He tipped his head on one side, and looked at her with those eyes, that could probably get anything they wanted if they tried.

"Oh, I just can't wait to see you tomorrow," she said to him, gave him a rub under the chin, then we both walked our own ways home.

That evening my mum seemed a little bit stressed as she was getting ready to go out to a social event, to meet some new friends. She kept rushing around.

"I know it's here somewhere," she kept saying.

"What have you lost Mum?" I asked. She just continued rushing around looking through everything. Eventually Scruffy began looking worried, almost like my mum's anxiety had transferred onto him as well! He began sniffing around, and eventually dived into the pile of shoes at the bottom of her wardrobe.

"Oh no Scruffy," my mum shrieked. Eventually he came out, with her purse in his mouth, like it was a fun toy to chew. "Wow! Thank-you so much boy" my mum said. My mum has a tendency to be a bit messy at times, and I don't know how that purse got in there, but it felt as if there was a big sigh of relief, as she seemed so pleased to be able to leave the house, even though Scruffy had seen that purse as a toy! I still wonder how exactly it got there, but our new doggy saved the day as far as I was concerned!

The next day, I met with Clare again at the entrance to the old graveyard with Scruffy. He seemed very excited to see her too. She gave Scruffy a big hug, wanting to show he was special too, and his little tail wagged as her hands rubbed the fluffy area under his chin. When I stood up, something seemed to catch his eye, and he rushed off, like a dart. Both Clare and I ran after him.

"He's probably just chasing squirrels," Clare said. He kept jumping in and out of the undergrowth, and then jumped headfirst into a mass of greenery, with a few flowers, that was perhaps once a grave.

"Scruffy" I shouted, "come here boy". Eventually his little head bobbed up, just like it had out of mum's pile of shoes. As he came out a bit more, it was evident he had something in his mouth. "drop it" I said, trying to remind him of the command I had practiced with him. Eventually, with the encouragement of a little tasty treat I carried with me in my bag, he put what he had into my hand, wagged his tail, and looked up, quite proud with what he had found.

Clare and I both looked down at what seemed to be a necklace. It appeared to be an oval gold pendant with some beautiful engraving across one side, hanging from a gold chain. I turned it over and gradually looked at it in my hand. There were pretty shapes on the front, possibly elaborate letters, intertwined in each other, but I wasn't sure what those letters were. Perhaps a V and a C? From the condition it was in, it must have been in the grass and brambles a very long time. Both Clare and I tried to look more closely at the area it had come from, and there was the base of a broken headstone, so the name of the buried person could not be read easily.

After a little looking around, I noticed there was a small blue wooden stake standing in the ground, at the base of the grave. I also remembered that a number of other graves had similar blue stakes, but we had never known why they were there.

"I wonder who this belongs to" I said to Clare.

"Well it's obviously been there a very long time, and I wonder what it is exactly." She responded.

"Maybe we should hand it into a lost property place," I said.

"Well I'm not really sure where there is one," Clare responded, frowning. I thought about it for a while, again looking at this dirty oval pendant on a chain.

"For the moment, why don't we just try and clean it up a bit, and then it might help us find the owner, if we can see it better." I responded. I put it into my pocket, possibly feeling a bit guilty, as a pigeon looked at me while it sat proudly on the top of another cross-shaped gravestone.

We then continued our walk, and after walking around the whole common playing fetch with Scruffy, we headed back to my house. Once we'd sneaked in through the front door, we took off our shoes, and tip-toed up to the bathroom. When we got there, I took out the find, and very gently cleaned the dirt off, pulling away all the small shrivelled leaves that had got stuck in the chain. Gradually it became more and more pretty as we cleaned away the dirt and pollen, along with old cobwebs.

"It does seem a bit odd, though," Clare said. "I mean, why have an oval gold piece, with a bit of engraving and that's it."

"Well I suppose it's a pendant" I said, and maybe they liked it like that in the old days". I felt all around it, then noticing that there seemed a tiny join along the side, which also seemed a bit odd. "Maybe it's made of two pieces of gold stuck together if it was too big to mould it from one piece of gold," I said, trying to find an explanation for the join.

"Just hide it" Clare said. "Don't tell anyone, maybe we should try and find out more answers, you'll help us won't you Scruffy!" she said, patting Scruffy on the head, who'd followed us up the stairs without me realising.

We decided to hide it in my bedroom, under the mattress for the moment, and then agreed a time to meet up the next day to take

Scruffy for another walk. He looked up at us with those special eyes, tongue hanging out, and tail wagging, saying yes in his own special way.

Chapter 15

When I woke up the next morning, I kept wondering whether finding the pendant had been a dream. I reached under my mattress, and grasped around, and yes! It was there! I pulled it out, then quickly pushed it back under as I heard my mum shouting my name out from downstairs. I then shoved a dressing gown on, and pushed the toothbrush up and down my teeth before rushing down for breakfast, looking at my watch. My brother was already downstairs before me, made a face at me as I jumped onto a seat. I gulped everything down as quickly as possible, as there wasn't much time left to get ready to meet Clare. Once finished, I rushed up to my room, threw on my clothes, and jumped into my trainers. Before long, I was rushing with Scruffy to the Common to meet my friend.

Scruffy and I jogged up to the common. He was jumping alongside me, kept looking up at me in excitement as though jogging there was a game for him. As we made our way up the road, I could see Clare waiting in the distance. I gave her a wave, and continued on.

"I'm really sorry", I said, as we ran up to her.

"Don't worry, let's go for a really fun walk!" She said. We walked on past all the flowers and overgrown grass, with a few brambles in the way. "Be careful of the stinging nettles," Clare said, pointing them out to me. As we moved through the old graveyard, to get to the common, Scruffy seemed very distracted. He kept pulling in the opposite direction, and wanting to go another way.

"What's wrong Scruffy?" I asked him. He gave a whining sound that seemed like he was worried, and eventually I gave in, and allowed him to lead us to a different part of the big old overgrown graveyard, which seemed to go on so far.

As we went on, I could hear some groaning, and Scruffy pulled even harder, sniffing around the ground like mad.

"Look" I said to Clare, as I could see there was an old lady, collapsed on the ground. We ran over to her, and Scruffy began running backwards and forwards between us and the woman, trying to tell us something. I gently shook the lady, who seemed virtually unconscious. "Are you ok?" I asked. The lady didn't say anything, but she seemed to be breathing.

"I'll call an ambulance" Clare said, getting out her mobile phone. In the meantime, we kneeled on the ground next to her, trying to get her name, but she didn't seem to know who or where she was. She had collapsed by a grave, with a yellow flower on it, and was wearing this very old- fashioned blue and white dress with a blue shawl. She was quite small, and the stick she perhaps used was lying next to her.   Eventually the ambulance came, and the paramedics thanked us for staying with her.

"Where will you take her?" I asked one of the team. "Southampton General Hospital" they told us, "probably an elderly care ward". They wanted to know if we were relatives. We had no idea how we could contact her family to let them know, as she didn't seem to have much with her, I wondered if maybe her handbag had been stolen. The ambulance men told us not to worry, and that they can work things like that out at the hospital.

After the ambulance men went, it felt like we had spent a large amount of time outside, but hadn't gone very far.

 "Oh well, we can still have a short walk" I said. We quickly walked through to the main park, and I asked Clare if she would be able to remember what the lady looked like, as we didn't know her name. Clare took out her phone.

"I know it might be a bit naughty, but I took a picture of her and a close-up of her face!" She said shyly.

"You never know, that may come in useful some time, I said, taking another glance at the small and withered features of her appearance, but at the same time knowing that 'selfies' and pictures in this situation were, maybe, a bit naughty. As we came towards the end of our walk, Clare gave Scruffy a big hug.

"If it hadn't been for you Scruffy, that old lady may never have been found, you are a very clever dog!" She said.

"I agree," I responded, and gave him a big hug too. His little tail wagged away, as he seemed to enjoy his praise.

Both of us made our ways home, and agreed to keep things a little bit secret, as we thought we might get told off for spending too much time out. As the evening went on. I couldn't stop thinking about the old lady. I sent a text to Clare, and asked if she thought we should go and visit her in hospital, as we didn't know if she had any family, and I felt a bit worried about her. She sent me a text back, and said she thought we perhaps should, but mentioned that it would require getting a bus, if we were going on our own. After that I went to sleep, checking the locket was still under my bed, which it was, thank goodness. My brother had not got his hands on it!

The next morning, I came down to breakfast, and Scruffy came bounding up to me after quickly eating his breakfast. He nuzzled my leg with his wet nose, as if he was asking for something. I gave him a big hug, and said that he may get a treat if he behaves himself! I then asked my mum if she would mind if I went to the hospital with Clare to visit a friend today on the bus. She looked a little reluctant, but agreed as long as we were back by 5pm, as Scruffy would need his dinner then. I quickly sent a text to Clare, letting her know. She asked her mum, and before long we were meeting up. I had placed the pendant in my pocket, as I was worried, that before long, my brother might find it, and start asking questions, or wanting to keep it for himself.

"Do you know how to get to the hospital?" I asked Clare. "Oh, it's easy, there's loads of buses. My sister works there." We were soon sitting on a bus that took us to what turned out to be a huge place!

"How on earth will we know where she is?" I asked.

"Well the ambulance men said it would probably be an elderly care ward. It felt so scary as the building was so large, with so many corridors, lifts and large open spaces. We had no idea where to go. Eventually after following lots of signs backwards and forwards, we managed to make our way to the elderly care wards. "Now what do we do, we don't even know her name?" Clare asked. I thought a moment.

"What about that picture you took? We could look around, and work it out. Only half the people can be women, surely, and it must be split into male and female sections?" Clare opened the picture, and we walked around a little, trying not to be noticed. One of the younger nurses asked what we doing, and if she could help. "We're looking for our grandma", I said,

"she looks like this" Clare said, pushing the phone picture straight into her face.

"Oh, she's just over there", the nurse said pointing towards the window. We thanked her, and moved in that direction, carefully looking at all the faces.

In the corner, by the window, there was the same lady, with a drip line running down into her arm, a fluid-filled bag hovering above her head. Above her bed the name Emily was written on a mini white board. We walked over to her, and I wasn't really sure what to say. As we approached her, she smiled.

"And who are you?" She asked.

"Well this is Clare, and I'm Lizzy" I said. "We came here to see how you are".

"Well that's a great honour," she said, "but why do I deserve it?"

"We, in-fact our dog Scruffy, found you unwell in the graveyard, and we called an ambulance to get you to hospital, as we were worried about you." The lady looked at us, at first unsure of what we said, but then it sunk in. She was very happy to see us.

"Well, I'm very grateful to you, and Scruffy," she said. "but what were two young people like you doing in a graveyard?" Clare explained we had been walking Scruffy, and he was very good at finding things, so liked investigating what was in all the long grass.

"I also think the graveyard is quite an interesting place as well," I said. The lady, who now confirmed her name was Emily, but said we could call her "Auntie Emily", told us that "It is an interesting place indeed!". Clare smiled and nodded. Both of us then found seats, and sat down by her bed.

"Do you know why it's interesting?" She asked.

"Well it seems perhaps abandoned, and many unusual gravestones are broken with lots of different pretty wild flowers and long grass and brambles growing everywhere." I responded.

"It may seem abandoned, but it holds a number of special people", she said. "Have you noticed that there are a number of blue wooden pegs stuck into some of the graves?" I nodded. "Well the graves of people in those graves are from people who died on the Titanic." I had heard of the Titanic, and knew there were films about it, but didn't know much about it. "It was a grand ship thought to be unsinkable that actually sunk on its first voyage a number of years ago. It originally set off from Southampton, so it has a number of connections with our city." The lady seemed very knowledgeable about the graveyard, and told us stories about some of the people buried there. As she talked on, I thought I would ask her about the pendant Scruffy had found, as she seemed to know lots of history about the graveyard. I carefully took it from my pocket, and hid it in my hand.

"Can I ask you a question?" I asked.

"Of course", she said.

"Well Scruffy found this pendant, in one of the blue pegged graves, and it seems very old and interesting. I showed her the pendant, and she smiled.

"Do you know what this is?" She asked.

"Well, I guess it's a necklace and a piece of jewellery," I said.

"Well this is called a locket." She turned the oval gold pendant in her hand and ran her fingers over the engravings on the front. "These are initials, VC, do you see?" We both looked over into her hands, "These are most likely someone's initials engraved into the gold." As she then moved it round in her hand, she showed us a little secret latch. "Now if you click this open…" The oval pendant then sprung open, on a hinge, almost like a book. As it opened, there were two black and white pictures, one on each side. On one side, the picture of a man dressed in old fashioned but very smart-looking clothes. On the other side a pretty young woman, from a similar era. Her clothes were also posh with a beautiful dress.

"Wow", I said. I was quite surprised how we had kept it all this time but did not realise there were pictures inside. "My brother is never getting his hand on this!" I said.

"It's so pretty" Clare said.

"People used to wear these to remember a loved one, and sometimes they kept a lock of hair, inside. I wonder who it is? Wouldn't it be exciting to know?".

"Auntie Emily, would you mind if we came to see you again before you go home?" I asked.

"Of course," she said. "My son is always so busy, I rarely get a lovely visit, especially from young faces" she said, smiling. "Sometimes this place could do with some freshening up!" She winked at us. She looked so much better than when we had found her at the graveyard. After that we said goodbye, and left to go back to the bus-stop. As we sat down, waiting for the bus, Clare and I chatted about our surprise with the locket.

"Would you be able to remember what grave it came from?" I asked.

"Possibly, maybe it would prompt our memory if we took Scruffy for a walk there again." Clare answered. Before long we had travelled on the bus, and it was then time for us to get off at our stop.

As soon as I got in through the front door home, Scruffy came bounding up to me, excited, sniffing and jumping around. He was so happy. He kept sniffing at my pocket where the locket was, pushing his wet nose against my leg.

"I don't know why you're so interested in that?" I smiled at him. "Dogs don't wear jewellery do they?" As I came further into the house my mum asked if we had a good time seeing my friend at the hospital. I said we had, and before I knew it, we were having dinner. I was just relieved my mum hadn't asked any further questions!

Chapter 16

The next day, Scruffy didn't seem so well, and he was sick a few times. I got quite worried about him.

"Maybe I should take him to the vets?" I asked my mum. I looked down at him, and he seemed so deflated, with his head on his paws, not wanting to move, or go for a walk. He wouldn't eat any food. My mum agreed, but said she needed to go the supermarket.

"If I give you the money, do you think you could go with your brother or even your friend?" My mum asked. We made an appointment, and I rung Clare who came with me. When the appointment came, and we were called into the vet's examination room, we both lifted Scruffy onto the vets table.

"Now who do we have here?" the vet asked. "Well this is Scruffy, and I'm worried, as he's been sick and won't eat anything. He just doesn't seem himself." The vet looked him over, looking in his mouth, ears, and just about everywhere. He then checked his temperature, and eventually said that just like humans, dogs can get tummy bugs too. He advised on some special dog food and gave him some medication to stop him from feeling sick. The vet advised that Scruffy should be offered plenty of water. Towards the end of his talk, Scruffy nudged my pocket, which had the locket in. I asked the vet if dogs like the smell of gold.

"No", the vet responded, laughing, his moustache rising above his mouth, pushing into his nose. "Dogs can be trained to sniff gold out, though, as their smell is so special", he said.

"Well it's just that Scruffy seems to like sniffing a piece of jewellery" I said.

"Well dogs are usually interested in something if there's an animal scent on it, or they want to guard it". The vet said. "Show it to me". I got the locket out of my pocket and put it in his hand. He raised his eyebrows, looking down at it. "Very interesting, rolled gold". Now he was beginning to sound like an antiques dealer! "Hmm". He opened the catch, opening the locket, and took a good look at the pictures inside. "Do you know anything about the people inside?" he asked.

"No, do you?" I asked keenly.

"I'm afraid not, but this is interesting." The vet pushed his finger into what looked look like the frame of the second picture, and opened the locket yet again, as though he was turning a page. As the small piece of metal opened further, containing the picture, it revealed a lock of black hair underneath. "Wow! This is like a little secret" I said.

"Looking at it, it doesn't look like human hair to me," said the vet. "It looks and feels a little bit more like animal hair, perhaps that's why Scruffy found it so interesting" he said, stroking then smelling it. "A real mystery. Well, I'll leave that mystery to you, as I really must move on, or I'll be in trouble" he said, quickly closing the locket, and handing it back to me with a smile showing all his shiny teeth under that big moustache.

As we walked out, with Scruffy's new food, I began feeling a bit guilty, as all I could think about was the locket, and who could be in it, and why there would be animal hair in it. But the whole point of going to the vets was to help Scruffy get better! I looked down at him.

"I'm sorry boy," I said. He tilted his head, and looked up at me as if he understood, somehow. Clare came home with me for a quick cup of tea. As we sat down with our mugs of tea, I asked her what she thought of the vet's discussion about the locket.

"I think tomorrow we should go back to the graveyard, and find the grave it came from, and take a picture." She said. "Scruffy will need a walk anyway if he's better. We could always ask Auntie Emily a bit more about the grave if we can't think of anything." "Ok, let's meet tomorrow at 9am at our usual place, outside the graveyard, and I'll let you know if Scruffy is still unwell," I said.

That night I couldn't stop thinking about the locket. Who were the people inside? Why would they want animal hair inside a locket? In the end, I sent a text to Isabelle, and we set up a secret live chat on skype. I hid myself and my computer under the duvet, so no-one would know I was still awake. I told her about the locket, where it was found, and what Auntie Emily had said, about the graveyard, and the way people from the Titanic were buried there. Isabelle became excited by the story, and said she thought the tragic sinking of the Titanic was such an interesting story, even if it was perhaps a bit overtold.

"Do you know they kept dogs on the Titanic?" she said.

"Dogs on a ship?" I asked, almost not believing her.

"Oh, yes, and some ladies were naughty and kept them in their cabins".

"How do you know that?" I asked.

"Well, I read about it when reading a leaflet about what happened to the ship when it sunk". Isabelle wasn't sure who the people in the pictures could be, but after we chatted for a bit about my new school, and what the summer holidays had been like in London, we both went to sleep. I didn't want to get in trouble for chatting on-line overnight!

The next morning, Scruffy managed to eat some of the food the vet had given us, and reluctantly ate his worming tablet as well. "Are you sure you should be taking him for a walk yet?" My mum asked.

"Well I promised Clare, and the fresh air might do him good," I said. My mum screwed up her eyes, and eventually agreed he could go with me.

When I saw Clare waiting, she came running over, and threw her arms around Scruffy.

"Are you feeling better boy?" She asked. Scruffy licked her face, so Clare took that as meaning yes! We walked through the graveyard, looking at the graves, especially keeping our eyes open for ones with blue wooden pegs sticking out. "Could it be this one?" Clare asked, pointing to one such grave.

"No, I think the one Scruffy found the locket in had a bigger stone, and it was sloping at a funny angle. It also had lots of bird poo on it, and was closer to the pathway," I explained. As we looked around, we eventually came to one, with a pigeon perching on the top. Scruffy went over to it, and seemed to have fun jumping into all the overgrown grass surrounding it. He eventually emerged, with lots of grass seeds all over him. "I think this is the one, I said. "It's got lots of bird poo on, and the funny green thing to put flowers in, but looks as though no-one's put flowers in for years."

We both crouched down and viewed the stone, which looked like it was going to fall over. It looked really old, and dirty. Clare got out her phone and started taking lots of pictures of it. I stood at the front and tried to take a picture of the name on the front. I wasn't one hundred percent sure, but I think it said 'In loving memory of Robert Chesterfield'. It said a few other things, such as maybe the date, and a few sentences about how he will not be forgotten, but it was so hard to read due to all the moss and bird poo. I hoped that we could make the pictures we had taken look bigger to help us.

After we had taken the pictures, Clare and I took Scruffy for a good walk, but were careful to make sure he looked well. We then both made our own ways home, and agreed to try enlarging pictures to try and work out more about the gravestone. As I came in through the front door, my mum had asked if Scruffy was alright?

"Oh yes, he feels better now", I said. "We still need to give him the special food though," just in case she thought I'd forgotten. Scruffy seemed to enjoy his dinner, taking good licks of water from his bowel afterwards. The little wet beard he always got afterwards, made his orange fur darker under the mouth, which always made me laugh.

Scruffy came with me up to my room that evening as I put the photos on my computer and enlarged them as much as I could. I got a pen out, and wrote down the name Robert Chesterfield, which I could just about see from the picture of the gravestone. I could also read that he died in 1912, and the word 'missed' and 'loved' also appeared among the mix of words that I couldn't quite read due to all the annoying moss. Could the man in the picture be Robert Chesterfield? I wondered. What was the relevance of the date? I thought about what to do.

"What do you think Scruffy" I asked. "You managed to find this strange piece of jewellery in that grave, is it trying to tell us something?" After that, I got ready for bed, and sent a text to Clare, asking if she'd managed to work anything out. She said she could read the name, but wasn't sure of much else. She said she would search on the internet to see if she could find any information. I sent her a text back asking if we should go and ask Auntie Emily. We both agreed to go and see her, if our mums' allowed.

The following day, we both went to the hospital, and took Auntie Emily a box of chocolates. As we handed them to her, her small face displayed a big smile. We showed her the pictures of the gravestone, and I read her what I had noted on the grave.

"Well", she said. "1912 is the year the Titanic sunk. This was a big disaster, as the ship was a very glamourous ocean liner said to be unsinkable. There were many rich people on board, and when this happened, there were not enough lifeboats. It still holds some mystery and wonder to people as it was such an exciting glamourous ship at the time, said to be not only 'unsinkable', but the biggest ship ever built at the time. Have you ever been on a large ship? "

"No, but my father goes to work on ships for long periods of time," I said.

"You should read about the Titanic" she said, "as many people lost their lives and it caused us to change the way we build and run a ship forever. It was also full of exciting glamour. Some people were also travelling on board it to emigrate to America forever, or so they planned.

Now, that name, 'Robert Chesterfield', I'm not sure I know that name, but I might know someone who may know a little more. She's one of my friends at my knitting class. I'm being discharged from hospital tomorrow, so perhaps I can introduce you when I come out of hospital."

"Oh, that would be great!" I said. With that we gave her our numbers, and she gave us hers. I turned round and a nurse was behind us, saying it was medication time, so we should be going.

"Oh these are my niece's nurse" she said.

"I thought they were your granddaughters?" The nurse said.

"Oh, how could I be so forgetful, of course" she said, giving us a wink. With that we left the ward, heading for home. As I got in that evening, and later sat down to dinner, my brother spoke.

"So what have you been up to?"

"Nothing", I said.

"Well, you've been away or in your room all the time."

"Nothing guys would find interesting."

"Well you wouldn't find what I've been up to interesting", he responded. My mum moaned that we should learn to help each other out rather than moan at each other. She then asked what we wanted for dinner. I managed to persuade her that fishfingers were the best option, so I got my way!

Chapter 17

The next day, I met with Clare again, and after taking Scruffy for a fun walk, I reminded her about what Auntie Emily had said about contacting her.

"Maybe we should give her one or two days to settle at home first" Clare suggested. "Why don't you come around to mine, and we can look up some info on the Titanic, to see if it can answer some of our questions?" She asked. Before long we were in Clare's bedroom, huddled around her computer screen. We had sneaked Scruffy up there, and made sure he had a pee first before taking him up. It was all very tidy, and painted lots of pretty pink colours. Her bed was perfectly made, with a teddy bear sat in the centre. "His name is teddy", Clare said, pointing to him.

"Well, we better not let Scruffy think he's a toy!" I said, thinking that could get us into trouble if he was a prized gift!

I looked at the computer screen and Clare typed 'Titanic' into a search. So much information came up. We didn't know where to start. We then refined the search slightly by typing history of the Titanic. Gradually by altering our search, and refining down information, it became more and more interesting. We learnt how The Titanic was the largest man-made ship built at the time, and had a massive crew of 900 people. It was very glamourous, with their second class the equivalent of our first class today! We learnt how it hit an iceberg, and sunk without enough lifeboats to carry everyone on-board. Even the lifeboats that were there were not filled properly! We read how over 1500 people died because of the sinking, with many sad stories connected. Clare told me about the SeaCIty museum, which was in our town, and we thought of visiting it, as it had a Titanic exhibition, which may tell us some more.

"So do you think VC could have been someone on the Titanic?" I asked Clare. "Well, it's quite possible, but then, how did the locket end up in the graveyard?" Later on, Clare and I had lunch, and before long it was time for me to take Scruffy home. My mum seemed happy that I hadn't come home too late, and that evening we watched the TV with some popcorn she had made as a surprise. I gave her a big hug, as sometimes my mum had seemed to recognise how much I loved popcorn, and I loved her surprises.

The next day, I got a phone-call from Auntie Emily, who invited Clare and I around, saying there was a friend she'd like us to meet.

"I know you'll be excited to see this lady" was how she ended the conversation after agreeing a time for the afternoon. She gave us her address, which was not far away from the Common. I then phoned Clare, and we decided to meet at the Common first to give Scruffy a walk beforehand. Auntie Emily had agreed that Scruffy would be welcome in her house.

Once Clare and I met, we began throwing balls for Scruffy so he could run around all the large amount of grass. He would bring them back, and drop them at our feet, looking up with a frown, as if to say 'you are going to throw another one aren't you?'. After finishing our quick walk, I took out the piece of paper I had written Auntie Emily's address on, and felt for my phone. I opened up my satellite navigation application, and typed in her postcode.

"That looks really cool", Clare said.

"I love it", I responded, "My dad showed it to me, and I persuaded him to let me download it just before we came down here, as I felt I didn't know how to get anywhere!" We followed the instructions it gave, and eventually came to a little detached house with a white door down a small side-street, not that far from where we were. Scruffy carried his favourite red ball all the way there, almost protecting it. "Should I knock on the door?" I asked.

"Look, there's a doorbell, I don't mind pressing it" Clare said. As she pressed it, it made a strange ring, resulting in Scruffy pinning his ears back. We waited a few moments, and then we could hear some very slow steps shuffling on the other side of the door.

It was so lovely to see Auntie Emily's smiley face and unbrushed bright white hair as she swung the front door open.

"Hello girls" she said, ushering us in. "Come in, do you want some tea? Ooh, look what special visitor we have today", she said, looking down at Scruffy, still holding the red ball in his mouth. Scruffy looked proudly up at her, as if displaying it like a trophy. We were moved through to the sitting room, where another old lady was sitting. She had a walking stick by her side, and white curly hair. Her skirt was a yellow colour, and looked quite formal, perhaps old fashioned.

"Hello", we said. Auntie Emily came in with a tray of teacups, the cups making a clunking sound as she shuffled along. She then sat down and began introducing us.

"This is Sophie Adams", she said. "Now girls, why don't you tell Mrs Adams the story you told me about what you found at a grave in the old graveyard." Gradually we explained the story of the locket, the pictures inside, and showed the pictures of the grave of Robert Chesterfield, where Scruffy had found the locket. I then showed her pictures of the locket I had taken.

"All this technology, I don't know, it's all a bit too much for me" Mrs Adams said. "But I think I might know a few exciting things."

"Yes?" both Clare and I replied in unison.

"Well, although my name is Mrs Adams, that's my marriage name. My maiden name is actually Chesterfield. I can also tell you that my grandmother was called Victoria," she said. "I think, though, I need to properly see the locket before I tell you any more information as I don't want to inappropriately excite you". I slipped my hand in my pocket, and pulled it out, as I had put it there to protect it from the possible snooping nose of my brother. As I put it into the hands of Mrs Adams, she gasped. She turned it over in her hand very slowly, her knobbly fingers sliding down to the catch. She opened it up, and as she looked at the pictures inside, she gasped. "This was my grandmother and grandfather". Victoria Chesterfield was my grandmother's name.

"You can open it up further, and there's some hair in the back" I said. Mrs Adams opened it up to look, as I was speaking. "You can see it's black, and we're not sure why, but our vet thinks it's animal hair" I told her.

"Oh, that's because it was probably from her dog" she responded. He was a black Newfoundland dog she loved very much called Nigel.

"Well we love Scruffy very much" I said, trying to show that we understood why someone would keep a bit of dog hair.

 "Well, her dog was very special, as he saved a number of lives when the Titanic ship sunk.

"Wow", I said.

Auntie Emily then told Mrs Adams about how Scruffy had really saved her, trying to make sure he didn't get forgotten about.

"So how do you think the locket ended up on the grave" I asked.

"Hmmm, well I'm not really sure, but I know that after my grandfather was buried there, I'm told my grandmother used to visit the grave frequently. She was always losing things, perhaps she dropped it there when putting flowers down. It's such a messy overgrown place, that it could get buried in the undergrowth I'm sure." Gradually, Mrs Adams took an old photograph out of her pocket, and showed it to us. "This was my grandmother in a very old crumpled photograph" she said. Looking at it, you could see the similarities in the pictures.

"Oh, this is all so exciting, isn't it girls" Auntie Emily said. I felt excited, as it explained the mystery of the locket a little, but I knew I would probably have to give it back to Mrs Adams. "We've found it very interesting", Clare said. "Before this, I didn't really know about the Titanic, only that it was a film, and now I've learnt so much. "There are more things I want to find out", I responded. "I wonder what it was like for Mr Chesterfield, it must have been very frightening". "I know this must mean a lot to you, to find an old piece like this with reminders of your grandmother, so you can keep the locket Mrs Adams" I said. She looked at the locket, rubbed it and thought about what I had said.

"We should be going soon as my mum will be moaning," I said. Mrs Adams handed the locket back to me. "It's your grandmother's, so you can keep it," I said.

"I want you girls to keep it, as it's not really much use to me, and there's no-one for me to hand it on to," she replied. I couldn't help smiling in almost relief, as I felt it was a very special piece of history we had discovered. Clare insisted on taking a picture of all of us, and after that, we went home. I felt that we had met a very kind-hearted lady.

As I got in, my mum looked pleased.

"I have something to tell you!" she said, wanting me to guess.

"It's fishfingers for dinner?" I asked.

"No, silly. You're dad's coming home for a break!" I felt pleased, but strangely as it seemed so long since we had seen him, and so much had happened, I felt guilty that I didn't feel over-excited. I went and told my brother, who seemed more interested in his computer game.

"Well aren't you pleased?" I asked.

"I suppose so" he responded. With that, I closed the door to his bedroom.

Later that evening, dinner seemed nicer, perhaps as my mum was so happy, and soon it was bedtime. I ensured the locket was hidden under my mattress and was soon ready to fall asleep. Over the next few days, Clare and I looked up more information about what kind of people were on the Titanic, and what happened when it sunk. To think that I had a piece of jewellery that had once been on such a special ship, and the hair of a dog that saved lives on the Titanic was visible in my hand as well!

Later that week, my dad came home. He knocked on the front door, with two large suitcases. I flung my arms around him as he came in.

"Group hug" My mum shouted as she joined in. She seemed so happy, and it got Scruffy excited.

"What is that?" My dad asked, pointing his finger at Scruffy, who had been barking at him as he approached the front door. Scruffy seemed to just keep barking, as though a dangerous stranger had broken into our home. "Well, answer me, what is that doing in our home?" My dad said.

"Come in love, and we'll tell you all about it". My dad looked very unhappy, as he picked up his suitcases to move up to his bedroom. As they went up, I could hear them arguing already!

After changing, he came down, and mum brought him a tea, as he sat in the main armchair.

"Well, how've you all been?" He asked, almost like he was just making conversation for the sake of it.

"We've been fine dad", I said. "We've met some new friends and mum's been really happy".

"I bet she has" my dad said. "You know you're not keeping it,", he said. "It was wrong of your mum to let you have a dog, especially without telling me, we don't have room for one."

"But dad, we've had him quite a while now, and he's settled into our home, it wouldn't be fair to..."

"This is not about fairness, it was not exactly fair getting it without asking me", he said. I could tell he really meant what he said, he was not joking. I pulled Scruffy towards me, and hugged him tight.

"You're not taking him away from us" I said defiantly, "He's my special friend, no, more than a friend, he's part of our home!" I said.

"Well, that's as may be, but he's going to have to go back now. My mum came and sat down. She stroked Scruffy, she then picked him up and touched noses with him.

"I know I should have discussed it with you, love, but I've grown fond of him too," my mum said.

"Well, he doesn't have to go back immediately, but he's going. You will ring the dog home tomorrow." I couldn't believe it. I was so angry, and upset I picked Scruffy up, and ran up to me room. I sat on my bed, still hugging our dog, feeling tears fun down my face, my cheeks were hot. I could feel my heart racing, and didn't want to come out of my room until my dad changed his mind.

After a while, I heard a knock on the door. My mum came in, and sat on the bed with me and Scruffy.

"You know he shouldn't really be on the bed don't you?" She said.

"I don't care", I responded. My mum waited for me to calm down, put her arm around me and gently explained that it wasn't what she wanted either, but it was for the best, and dad would never have allowed it in the first place, and it was all her fault. I eventually agreed with her, but couldn't accept it. That night, I told Clare all about what my dad had said, and that he wouldn't let us keep Scruffy. As I explained how upset I was, I played with my hair, trying to think what life would be like without him.

"Try not to be upset" she said. "Sometimes mums and dads do things that seem mean at the time but are for a good reason in the long term."

"I know," I said, "but I just don't understand what the problem is, Scruffy's done nothing wrong."

The next day I just couldn't talk to my dad. I ate breakfast without saying a word to him, as I was just too angry he could take my special friend away from us. My dad just gave me a look to suggest he did not approve of my behaviour. My brother seemed to continue playing his computer games, and gave the impression he didn't want to get involved. Somehow, though, I could sense he wasn't happy with my dad either. Because there was so much bad feeling in the house, 'phoning up the dogs home' managed to get delayed, until my dad mentioned it two days later at dinner again.

"Have you phoned that dog's home up" he asked as we sat eating. We could all tell he was still quite serious about it. My mum gave Scruffy a stroke on the head, and his little brown eyebrows raised up in the centre, looking up at her, as though he could sense something was not quite right.

"I suppose we'll do it in the morning", my mum said, in a deflated manor. The truth is, she had become quite fond of our doggie. I gave him a tickle under the chin, looking up at my dad, as Scruffy then rolled over requesting a belly rub. I looked up at my dad's face, but he didn't seem interested. When we went to bed later that evening, I pulled out the locket from under the mattress, turning it over in my hand, and thought how we would not even have had this little treasure, if it were not for Scruffy.

Chapter 18

The next morning, as we sat at breakfast, Scruffy suddenly sat bolt upright, then ran to the door, barking. As a letter came through the door, he started pulling at it, and ran towards me with it in his mouth as if in victory. I pulled it from him, and saw it was addressed to me! This was a surprise, as I wasn't expecting anything. I opened it, and noticed the paper had a big blue cross at the top. As I read down the lines, it stated that Scruffy had been nominated for a 'Blue Cross Pet Hero award' for his achievement and bravery, and this would be awarded by Southampton Lord Mayor the following week in the Town Hall. It also mentioned times to arrive, and that photographs would be taken. I read it again, as I couldn't believe what I had just read! I then went into the kitchen, and told both mum and dad, who looked very surprised. Robert screwed up his face.

"Pet hero award?" he questioned.

"Well, you don't know what he's achieved" I said. I then told my dad how he had alerted us to a collapsed elderly lady, and he'd stayed with us at the time, and saved her life. "We can at least keep him until he gets his reward can't we dad?"

"I suppose so", he said, with eyebrows raised.

Later that day I told Clare all about it. I was so excited about the award, I could hardly wait to get all the information out.

"Calm down," she said laughing, as I spewed the words out over the telephone. I gave Scruffy a special hug as I was so proud of him, and he wagged his tail as if an acknowledgement.

"How do you think this came about, though, and the mayor to give the award?"

"I guess Auntie Emily must have said something". She replied.

"You will come to the awards event, won't you?" I asked Clare.

"Of course" she said. That evening, I also told Isabelle all about it, and she was so happy!

It didn't seem to take long before the award ceremony came about. Mum managed to persuade dad that we could at least keep Scruffy until the awards were done.

"They're taking special pictures!" she told him. The hall was in the town centre, and we drove down there. That night we washed Scruffy in the bath, and brushed him, attempting to dry him with a hairdryer, which he didn't like very much. As I hugged him, I could still smell the nice blueberry coat conditioner we had used, and I had bought (or persuaded mum to buy). As we came into the town hall, we were directed to our seats, and sat down. Scruffy curled up under my seat, like he often did if there was a crowd of people. A lady came over to us and explained how when Scruffy's award was announced, we should go up to the stage for the mayor to give Scruffy his award. It all felt very formal.

The ceremony began thirty minutes after we arrived. I began to worry if Scruffy might need a pee! I quickly looked behind me to see if Clare was there. She'd sent me a text to say she'd arrived and was sitting towards the back. I could just about see her, so waved. She waved back, smiling. A man from the Blue Cross then began talking, explaining to everyone the importance of the Pet Hero ward. I could hear movement of camera men, who were taking pictures, and doing some filming. I then started feeling nervous, as it was quite official. "you've been awarded something very special Scruffy" I whispered to him.

"And this year we award Scruffy of Southampton an Animal Hero Award, for saving the life of Mrs Emily Procter" the speaker stated.

"Well go up then", my mum said, in a hurried manner. I walked with Scruffy up onto the stage, step by step. The mayor was standing next to the speaker. He handed me a framed certificate, and then placed a little blue cross medal around his neck. The mayor then bent down to me and whispered in my ear

"Look after him well as he's very special".

"I will", I whispered back. I couldn't stop smiling, I felt so happy and proud. It was almost as if my heart was going to explode out of my chest, it was beating so fast! All the people in the room were clapping, it felt so special, like we were famous! I stroked Scruffy's head, and then gradually walked back down the steps with him back to our seat. We watched as some more awards were given, and then went to a gathering for some drinks and nibbles.

Clare came over to me once we got a drink.

"I've got some great pics!! She said. "Can't wait to show you". I laughed, as she pointed to her pink camera. As we stood having a few drinks, the mayor came up to us, smiling.

"Hello sir," he said to my father. "You must be proud".

"Well I...." Before my father could finish his sentence, the mayor interrupted and said

"Your dog saved my sisters life, I commend you on training him so well". He patted my father on the back, with a manly smile. My father looked rather pleased with himself. I thought it was all a bit ridiculous really, as Scruffy wasn't really his dog! Oh well, I guess that's an adult thing.

"Don't you think Scruffy looks brilliant?" Clare asked my dad, showing my dad her pictures of us up on the stage. He couldn't help smiling, and nodded.

We continued to chat, speaking to a few of the other dog owners who'd won awards. One dog peed on the floor, accidently. Well that was their fault for taking so long to start the ceremony, I think! Scruffy was very good, he managed to hold himself until I took him out.

"I'm proud of you boy" I said as he relieved himself on the grass patch outside. He looked at me, wagging his tail as if he understood.

When we got home, we all sat down. I felt quite tired, as it had all been a lot to take in. I sat down on the sofa. Scruffy lay down next to me, putting his head on my lap, his little wet nose slightly dampening my skirt. I giggled, as it had become a comforting thing. My hands played with the blue cross award around his neck. As my dad sat down too, I looked at him, stroked Scruffy's head.

"You're not going to make us get rid of him now are you?" I asked, looking up at my dad.

"No, I suppose he's earned his special place in our family" he said with a smile. I felt so relieved from then on. It was as if a weight of worry had been lifted away. The last few nights I had been trying to plan all kinds of ways we could keep Scruffy. I had even thought of running away and hiding with him at one point! I knew that was stupid, though.

The next day, I thought about my dad, and the way he really did not seem to want us to keep a dog, and that I should thank him properly, and maybe talk to him a little, as before he had been away for quite a long time at work, and talking on the phone just isn't the same thing as speaking in person. After my mum went out to get some groceries, I knocked on the door to his bedroom, and asked if we could chat, sitting down on his bed.

"Yes, chat away", he said.

"I just wanted to thank you a little for agreeing to let us keep Scruffy," I said.

"Well, I can see he's a special dog, and it seems lots has gone on here while I was away at work" he said. "Tell me a little bit about Scruffy, how you found him and what makes him a special dog" he said, looking at me with interest in his eyes, almost for the first time since he'd come home.

I told my dad about the old graveyard, how we had found Scruffy there, and how it was so interesting as some people who were on the Titanic were buried there. I told him about how Scruffy enjoyed it there as he likes searching for things, and was good at finding unusual things (including mums purse). I mentioned about how he had alerted us to Auntie Emily, and helped save her, but dad kind of already knew that story because of his award.

"So are you interested in the Titanic?" My dad asked.

"Well, I didn't know much about it until I visited the old graveyard, and Clare and I found out more about it, dad" I said. "It's made me wonder more about that ship, though, and how it must have been something very special", I said.

"Oh, it definitely was", my dad said. "Now, would you like to learn more about it?" he asked. I nodded my head. "Well, did you know in Southampton there's a large museum pretty much dedicated to the history of sailing and the sea, showing you lots of information. Would you like to go?" Normally, the thought of a museum can sound a little boring, but this sounded like something slightly different. "It can be something we can do together, just us, a father and daughter thing if you like?" At first I thought he was just trying to avoid the cost of another ticket for my brother, but as I looked at him, I could see it was something he really wanted to do with just me.

"I'm looking forward to this, dad" I said. That evening, my dad mentioned that both of us would be visiting the SeaCity museum and Titanic exhibition in it the following day. My brother screwed his face up a little bit as he munched his food.

 "Sounds a bit boring to me" he said.

"Well you don't have to come if you don't want to" I said. My brother confirmed he was happy to keep himself occupied with other activities, and that was that.

In the evening I phoned Clare to tell her my dad and I were going to the SeaCity museum to see the Titanic exhibition. She wanted to come too, but even if my dad had been keen for her to come, she couldn't anyway as her grandma was visiting for dinner. We chatted about some of the cool pictures she had taken, and some music clips we had both seen on youtube. We agreed to take Scruffy for a walk together at the end of the week, and after I put the phone down, I felt lucky to have such a good friend. When I went to bed that night, I found myself wondering what the museum would have on display, and whether it could tell us any more about people buried in the old graveyard.

Chapter 19

The next morning, I put on my favourite jeans, which had a little bit of a tear in them (but I hadn't told anyone), and a nice bright t-shirt. My dad made me change and put something a bit smarter on. He was happy with me wearing a skirt and shirt, which I didn't feel was necessary. I then grabbed my bag and phone. I gave Scruffy a little hug and told him we would be back soon, then we were in the car and on our way. It didn't take long to get to the museum, which seemed huge! It was almost like three concrete triangles lying on their sides, each one growing out of the next triangles' base.

"You know once upon a time this was a court and a police station" my dad said.

"Well at least it's got a nicer job now", I replied.

As we walked into the museum, everything looked so large. There were large posters and drawings explaining how grand a ship the Titanic was. There was a wall, with a list of all the crew that died on board. As I looked down the list, one name stuck out to me-Robert Chesterfield, listed as an 'Able bodied seaman'. I thought about the picture in the locket, and the picture of the face on the wall, I almost couldn't believe that I had been able to see a piece of history that had been hidden for so long in that locket. As we walked around the museum, there were various pictures, some original film footage taken when the Titanic was leaving Southampton all those years ago in black and white, which was fascinating, I found some original artefacts and pieces even more exciting, as you could imagine how people all those years ago had touched or seen the same pieces. As we moved around, I felt more and more fascinated with each piece of information, and little antique (even a pocket watch that had stopped at the time the ship sunk!) Part of me then thought about the locket, all the history it held, and how I had it, and no-one else really got to see it. Was this fair? It meant a lot to me, as it was a special thing Scruffy had found, and really how we had met Auntie Emily.

"So are you enjoying the display?" My dad came up behind me and whispered into my ear, giving me a bit of a shock.

"It's amazing dad," I said.

"Well, I thought it's been a long time since we've done anything together, and you deserved a treat. I'm surprised you've enjoyed it so much, that's nice to know." It's funny, as it was only a small thing my dad had said, but it meant so much to me. This made me smile as we left the museum.

As I lay in bed that evening, I couldn't stop thinking about the locket, and whether it was right I should be the only one to see it. What could I do about that anyway? I still felt pleased at how clever Scruffy was to have found it. Gradually I turned over in the bed, pulling the duvet over my head, to block out the light from my digital alarm clock, and fell asleep.

The next morning, I met with Clare, to walk Scruffy.

"Do you think other people should see the locket?" I asked as we walked through the old graveyard, Scruffy jumping in and out of the undergrowth, every so often showing his ginger head above some stinging nettles.

"Well Scruffy found it, and who else would you give it to?" Clare asked.

"Well, I don't know, but it's a part of Titanic's history, well almost, and I can't tell you how enjoyable it was to see the items on display at the Titanic exhibition with my dad."

"Well I suppose so, but I'm not really sure how you can give it to someone else?" Clare asked.

"Oh, I don't know, maybe it's a silly idea" I said. I didn't talk about it any more, but that evening I still couldn't stop thinking about it.

In the evening I looked at the SeaCity museum's webpage, and read about how they had come across some of the antiques, as well as a section on donations. I then thought that maybe I should donate the locket. As long as I could still see it, like other people could, then that would be fine. I also thought about how really it was Scruffy, though, who'd found the locket. I sat down at my desk, and took out some paper and a small jiffy bag I'd had in my drawer for quite a while. I began writing a letter to the SeaCity museum, explaining what the locket was, where it'd been found and the history I had discovered, including the man in the picture being Mr Chesterfield. I didn't really want people at school to know I had found it, though. I said in the letter that I wanted it to be displayed so everyone could see it, as it was special. I then looked at the pictures of Scruffy with his bluecross medal, and put a picture of him inside the jiffy bag, just to show how special the finder of this piece of jewellery was. I felt that by making the letter and donation anonymous, people at school wouldn't make fun. There was only a picture of Scruffy that may connect me. I checked the address for the museum on-line, and wrote this onto the small jiffy bag. At first I wasn't quite sure how to send the bag, and thought the best option was to go the post office, so they could arrange this.

The next day, my mum asked if I could pop down to the nearest small shop to get us some milk. She seemed surprised that I was keen to do this, but I saw this as an opportunity to pop to the post office, which was close to the shop. I went alone, and walked in. As I opened the door, an old-fashioned bell jingled to the post office. There was a queue, mainly of older people, some of whom seemed to be discussing things with the lady at the desk for ages! As we waited, the old lady in front of me looked at me, raising her hand up, showing me some kind of card.

"Pension withdrawal takes far too long" she said, almost as if she could tell I was frustrated with timing. She patted her hands against her hair, as if making sure her grey and white hair was tightly curled against her head in a perfect way, and no hairs were out of place.

"Maybe they need an extra helping hand and one person is not enough to deal with so many people", I said. I perhaps felt sorry for the lady serving who was dealing with an older person arguing at her.

"I agree," the lady said. Eventually I got to the front of the queue, and placed the small jiffy bag onto the desk in front of a glass panel. The lady behind the panel asked me to place the package on the scales, which I did, and then asked me to pay two pounds fifty. After paying, I pushed the package under the glass panel, through the lower slot, and soon it was officially in the post!

I began walking home, and just as I put my hand on the front door, I realised I hadn't bought any milk! As walked in, my mum asked for it. I had to pretend the shop didn't have any green top bottles. My mum did not approve, and said I should have bought a blue top bottle instead. I'm not sure whether she could tell I was not telling the truth, but she certainly seemed annoyed. It made me feel quite bad.

"I guess dad will have to wait until lunch-time for his cup of tea then, until I can get some milk" mum said.

Later that afternoon, I called Isabelle, and we had a chat on-line. It seemed ages since I'd seen her, and so much had happened. As she chatted, she twiddled with her hair, and told me about how she was beginning to get bored, as the summer holidays were quite long.

"Well, we'll be back at school soon" I said.

"I don't know whether I like the sound of that or not!" Isabelle responded.

"Well, you never know, it's a new school year isn't it, it might be more exciting," I said. As we chatted, we talked about some new films that were being released, as well as a new song released by her favourite singer. We listened to it together on youtube, and sang along, laughing. Towards the end of the conversation, Isabelle told me how much she missed me. I missed her too, and wished she could move to Southampton and perhaps meet my new friend Clare.

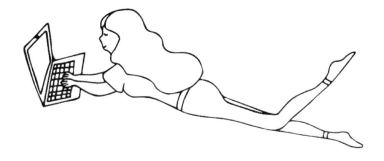

Chapter 20

It didn't seem too long before we were back re-starting school. It was a strange feeling, as I had only attended my new school for a short time before breaking for the holidays, and now I was back again. Clare and I managed to sit together on the first day, starting with science lessons. Our teacher, Mr Spencer, loved pointing to the big blocks of the enlarged periodic table, as he explained what it was, and what the numbers and letters meant. His beard always made me think about how often he must have to trim it to keep it so perfectly shaped. It was almost as if he was growing perfectly shaped hair on his face because there was not much on his head, just one very fine set of hairs scraped across his virtually bald scalp from one side to the other.

Later that day, my French lesson reminded me that I needed to practice my languages some more, as my mind was straying, and I couldn't help doodling on a scrap of paper, as our teacher Madamme Bisset talked on, and on, and on about La Rochelle, which was where she said she was from. The twins sitting in front of me kept whispering to each other, and I thought how that would annoy me if I was a teacher. Perhaps I was just in a bad mood! Towards the end of the day, it was nice to have a lesson with Mrs Crane, as I remembered how she had made me feel welcome on my first day. It reminded me how I had actually started at the school and provided some familiarity with her friendly voice.

As the week went on, I got into the same routine I was used to when school starts, of getting up, arguing over who uses the bathroom first, scoffing my breakfast quickly with Robert, and then getting out to school. It was strange, as so much had gone on in the Summer holidays, but I was already forgetting about it, as school can seem so busy, sometimes rushed. At the end of the week, my mum said she wanted to cook a special dinner for us as a family. I wasn't sure whether this was to celebrate something, or whether my mum had been watching a special cooking programme and wanted to try cooking their recipe. On Friday evening, I came into the kitchen after school, and my mum looked rather stressed.

"Now, I need the kitchen tidy, don't go leaving empty glasses on the side" she said. I was getting hungry, so I was trying to pick at something, but my mum quickly ushered me away, saying I needed to wait for my dinner, and she needed space.

After one hour, my mum called us down to sit at the table. She brought out a steaming hot homemade shepherds pie, and a large bowl of vegetables that included my favourite petit pois peas. Wearing her favourite oven gloves (that looked rather worn out, and had made their way over from our old house's kitchen), she set the food down, looking at my dad as if seeking his approval. My dad sat back in his chair, took a deep breath in, to savour the smell, and grabbed a serving spoon. Before long we were tucking into the meal. My dad loved shepherd's pie, so I knew he would be pleased. We chatted about what starting term had been like, and then towards the end of the meal my dad said he needed to talk to us about something. I felt slightly anxious at the tone of his voice. He then went on to say that he would soon have to go away back to work. I felt quite upset about this, as the time he'd spent at home had gone so quickly.

"Do you really have to go away again?" I asked, as if suggesting his job was not the best.

"I'm afraid so, darling" he said. "I will have to leave on Monday, but we've had a nice holiday, haven't we?" he asked.

"Of course, and Scruffy's loved seeing you" I said, giving Scruffy a stroke on the head as he lay under my chair. My dad rubbed the designer stubble on his chin, then gave me a hug, and moved his finger over to Scruffy. Scruffy sniffed it, as if approving that it was ok to invade his personal space.

My mum and I then spent Saturday shopping in the town. She bought me one of my favourite smelly candles in the town, almost to acknowledge that it was time for dad to go back to work. That evening, we all watched a film together, it was more one for the guy's, with action and a bit of violence thrown in! My brother and dad enjoyed it, but after a while, I found the film boring, but still wanted to sit with everyone. I found the internet more interesting, and looked at some of the latest fashions on the highstreet, as well as some Instagram pages on my ipad to stay occupied.

As I got ready for bed that night, I lit my candle, and took a deep breath to enjoy the lovely smell of roses it emitted. I found the sense of a candle so relaxing, for some reason. I'm not sure whether it was the dim lighting and flickering flame, or the special smell that made me feel that way, but I just loved it. I took a picture, and sent a text to Clare, boasting about how I had the best smelling candle burning, blew it out, like someone famous, then fell asleep!

Chapter 21

The next morning, I came downstairs for breakfast a little later than usual, and found my dad with a cup of tea reading the paper. He gradually sipped it, then flicked over a page, folding it over on itself.

"The Southampton Echo is quite good for a local paper" my dad said.

"Well not many people read a paper newspaper anymore, dad", I said.

"Well what do they read?" he asked, raising his eyebrows. "Do they just watch the news and that's it?"

"No, dad, all of this stuff can be read on-line now, why waste paper?"

"That's silly, it's recycled paper, I think, well, feels recycled anyway".

"Will you two stop arguing" my mum said.

I put the kettle on, and some bread in the toaster. I then got out some margarine, and honey. I was very tempted to take some chocolate spread, but, as usual, my brother had eaten it all! Once I 'd made up my breakfast, I sat down, and started to enjoy some lovely honey covered toast. My dad continued to read the paper.

"That's just rude dad" I said, a little bit annoyed that he seemed more interested in the paper than me! In fact, my dad seemed very interested in something in there!

"Hmmm", he mumbled, rubbing his chin. "That's unusual".

"What, dad".

"Well, do you remember the SeaCity museum, Titanic exhibition".

"Yes, dad".

"Well apparently they had an anonymous donation this week".

"How much money?" my brother asked, "I bet it was loads, they should have given it to me!"

"Rubbish" I said.

"No, it wasn't money".

"Well what was it then?" my mum asked.

"Well, it was a locket containing pictures of someone who was on the Titanic. It 's really unusual, as it has original pictures inside, and some dog hair! Apparently it has an estimated value of over twenty thousand pounds, perhaps more". As my dad read down the article, he went on to read how the dog hair was believed to be from a legendary Newfoundland dog who rescued some people when the ship was sinking. As he came towards the end of the article, his eyes then seemed fixed on some pictures alongside the article. "Well, I suppose jewellery is valuable, but it's only a small thing" my dad said. "Isn't that odd?" he said, eyebrows raised.

"yes?"

" There's a picture of a dog like Scruffy there as well, I don't think that's a Newfoundland". As he read further through the article, he noted that the picture was sent with the piece of jewellery.

"Let me read it?" I said, about to pull the paper off him.

"I thought you said newspapers were no longer required".

"Well, I suppose they're worth reading sometimes," I said. After my dad finished reading the paper, he handed it to me, with a slight smile on his face.

I felt so pleased, as I looked at the article, at least I knew for sure now the locket had got to the right place, where I wanted it. I looked down at Scruffy, who was sniffing around the floor, looking for crumbs. He looked up at me, raising his eyes almost begging for a piece of my toast.

"You did it boy", I said. He tipped his head on one side, as if trying to work out what I said, then carried on sniffing around the floor.

After I had eaten my breakfast, I took the paper up to my room and put it under the side-table next to my bed, safe, in a slightly hidden place. Robert was going off to football practice, so I knew it would be safe from him for today at least, but then I thought I might look at the SeaCity website later to see if there were any better pictures. I opened the website on my computer, and clicked on 'latest news and information'. As this page gradually opened, a box showing a picture of the open locket, with a blown-up picture of Scruffy next to it was on display in a cabinet. There was a small paragraph underneath headed 'Our latest discovery'. The paragraph stated the artefact was donated by an anonymous donor. I thought, as I read it, that it was written almost as though the locket had been donated by someone elderly or even someone who had stolen it, and now wanted to give it back. The picture of Scruffy, sitting upright next to it was special. If you looked carefully, you could see the blue-cross medal around his neck, but I knew that not that many people would know what that was or what it meant. I couldn't help stroking Scruffy as I clicked on the scrollbar to read on. "My special doggie", I said, "we know what it means".

Later that evening, we had another family meal, and this time it was a takeaway. I think they are more fun really! My mum chose the film we watched afterwards, and it was better than when Robert chooses. Before long it was bedtime. I went to bed perhaps a little earlier than normal, as I knew my dad would be leaving very early in the morning, before I left for school, and I wanted to make sure I said goodbye to him.

Having to wake up, the next morning, to the high-pitched ring of my phone's alarm was not enjoyable, though. I wanted to turn it off, and role over back to sleep, but managed to force myself to get up. When I went downstairs to breakfast, I found my mum and dad in a hug, which was nice to see, as so often in the past, I seemed to walk in on them arguing. My mum looked up at me as I came in, and asked if I wanted a cup of tea. I said I did, so she moved over to the kettle. My dad came over to me, and said that he would have to leave soon. In the corner of the kitchen I could see his packed suitcase, ready for him to go away again. This made me feel sad, as I felt closer to my dad since he had come home, even though he didn't like Scruffy at first.

My mum handed me a cup of tea, and a piece of toast, which surprised me. It also had some chocolate spread on (which was a real surprise as she must have bought it without telling us). As I crunched into the toast my dad sat looking at me.

"I just want to make sure we say goodbye properly" he said. "And a special goodbye to Scruffy too" he also said, as he gave him a pat on the head. This seemed funny, as when he first came home, he didn't want us to keep our special friend!

"That's ok dad, we know you have to go to work" I said.

"I said goodbye to Robert last night, so he doesn't need to get up early" my dad said, looking at my mum, as if to tell her that this conversation was between us.

My dad then gave me a big hug, after I finished my toast and tea. As he did this he whispered in my ear.

"I know what you did, and it's something I'm very proud of you for". He then looked at me with deep sincerity in his dark brown eyes, and gave me a big kiss on the cheek. He walked over to his case, picked it up, and took it over to the front door, with his car keys. My mum went with him, watched him get into his car, waving as he drove off, then closing the front door. Inside I could feel a lovely feeling of warmth that was so nice.

It was strange, as before I'd never felt so close to my dad, often angry with him like when he first arrived home. His stay home, though, had brought us together. It was almost like he understood what was important to me, and why. My mum came back to the kitchen, asking what dad had said to me. "That's a father to daughter secret", I said. My mum frowned, almost in surprise, then ushered me to go and get ready for school.

As I got ready in my bedroom, Scruffy came in, pushing the door open with his ginger paw, sniffing my leg, then lying down, placing his head on his paws, looking up at me, with his doggie frown. I couldn't help looking at him, then at the blue cross I had put framed onto my wall. I thought about how really, without Scruffy, none of all the special things that had happened since we'd lived in Southampton would have occurred. He had become my forever friend who I knew would always be there for me no matter what. As he sat up, Scruffy gave me his paw, in a 'payshake' which was a new trick he seemed to have learnt. He then looked up towards me with those special eyes.

"Good boy", I said, knowing that this simple statement was enough to help him know that he was special to me, and we were a special team no matter what!

TheEnd

Printed in Great Britain
by Amazon

79855014R00061